BOOKS FROM KAOTIK COW

OUTLAST SERIES

GEEKS WILL GATHER

GEEKS WILL RISE

GEEKS WILL FALL

OUTLAST YOUTH

ALLEN AND BRANDI VISIT ZOMBIEVILLE

Book One & Two

JOHN PARKS NOVEL

VETERANS AFFAIRS

OUTLAST:

Geeks Will Rise

By Shane Michael Lassetter

An Open Dialogue

Howdy do to all my loyal geeks. This book is a little shorter than the last one. Reason: only five days long because I wanted to finish it on Halloween night. Read on to find out why. Part of the explanation will be in the next book, too. *'Geeks Will Rise'* is titled this way because more groups are coming together and becoming part of the whole. Enough spoilers.

Thank you once again to everyone that is enjoying my ramblings. I really have fun with these books, even when I have a problem coming up with the words. Always my love goes to my wife, Cindy, and my two boys, Lucas and Zachery, first. Thank you to my friends that encourage me; Asdrubal, Warren, Renee & Dylan Bertram, and those I have met on the road. That is all. Enjoy.

Chapter 1

3am, Saturday, October 26th

Brazoria County, TX.

"Mayday! Mayday! This is Officer Turbin of the Pearland P.D. Anyone read? Mayday! Mayday!" He waited one minute. Maybe.

"Mayday! Mayday! Someone please answer! This is Officer Turbin of the Pearland Police Department. Can anyone hear me? Wake the hell up, please!"

"Hello? This is Perry. What's wrong?"

"We're under fire at the station. Unknown number of assailants. We need help! Now!"

"Well, shit. I can't help you. I'm in a wheelchair in Rosharon. Anyone else out there?"

"This is Sherriff Ingram. Alvin Police Department. I can send a squad car but that's it. We're depleted of officers ourselves here."

"Damn! That's not gonna do it. We're under heavy fire. I'm talking military firepower. Shit, is there anyone else? I don't even know who's shooting at us. We had no warnings."

"This is Private Henry of the U.S. Army, sir. I'm down in Lake Jackson. We've got the men and firepower, but it would take some time to get to you."

"ASAP, son. As in 'Get the Fuck Here Now'! Please. I've got civilians in here and only five officers. I don't know how long we can hold out."

"I'll get my C.O. and get right back to you, sir. I promise we'll be coming."

"Please hurry." An explosion could be heard before Turbin released the radio button.

"Sir?" No response. "Sir, are you still there?" Still no response. He sent another man to wake Major Bertram Bharata. He was the man in charge of their many military men. While waiting, he kept trying to get back in contact with the officer.

"Major. Major!" The Private knocked on the doorframe of the room he was sleeping in. "Wake up sir. We have an emergency."

As soon as the word emergency was out, Bert was up and awake while Rosalita stirred next to him. "What is it?"

"Pearland Police Department, sir. They are under heavy fire and request assistance. They have civilians and don't know where or who the fire is coming from."

"Wake everyone. Quickly. Watch yourself around the Seals though. They rise quickly and ready for war."

"Yes sir."

Before Bert could get fully dressed and outside, the Seals were standing out front; geared up and ready for war. Those boys were always ready to fight the good fight. Even with partial hangovers from the night before. It had been a night to celebrate the coming together of their Corpus Christi group with the ragtag band forming in Lake Jackson. One week into the Zombie Apocalypse and America was already reforming. Slowly.

"Men, I don't have all the details, but we need to move. People in Pearland are under fire. Police and civilians. Private, do we have any more information?" By this time, most of their large group was out front to hear why everyone was being awoken from a great night of bar-b-que, alcohol, and new friendship.

"Not much sir. We lost contact before I came to get you and can't get anyone back. Officer Turbin of the Pearland P.D. said it was an unknown number of assailants with heavy firepower. We heard an explosion before we lost contact. That's it, I'm afraid, sir."

"Alright." He looked directly at his deadliest of warriors. "Seals. Mount up. Every man and woman that can fit into a Humvee and the Deuce and a Half, get moving. I'll call over to our birds and have them wind up." He looked over to his Cobra pilot. "Tommy. You and Pete get your ass moving and get your birds in the air. I want both of you heading that way now. Get there quickly and assess the situation. Load up for hell on earth. Go."

"I'm going with you of course. I know you're not planning on staying here. It isn't in you." Rosalita Hernandez grinned at him. She was Bert's girlfriend. Well. Now she was. They never went out before Zombiegeddon but found their like for each other since and were primarily inseparable.

"Wouldn't have it any other way. We might need your nursing skills too. On top of your shooting."

"With that in mind, I'm going in right behind y'all. I think we should take the medical helicopter we acquired. I have a bad feeling." Gerald 'Gerry' Tannert spoke up. He was a retired Navy pilot and the only one the Lake Jackson group had until Bert and the others met up with them.

"Damn good idea Gerry."

"I'm going too. I'll ride with him and look over the inventory on the way." Michelle, a former nurse until she had her recent addition and chose to stay home to raise the baby, chimed in.

"Well shit. If my wife is going to insist on going, count me in" said William Pendale.

"We're going too. Maybe we can help the pilots find their way. We know Pearland and where the police station is." Steve Hull and Davis Masters volunteered. Steve was former Marine Force Recon and Davis was a former Army Ranger.

"Okay, load up and stop yapping already." Bert was happy so many wanted to help. He didn't have it in him to make people go. There was no telling what was awaiting them. "Rosa, can you grab everything and get us ready? I'm going to radio for our big bird to take some of us ahead of the vehicles. This sounds pretty urgent."

"Roger, roger." Rosa said in her best imitation of a droid from Star Wars.

Smiling, Bert called the Chinook that was sitting at the Super Wal-Mart. "Billy, I need you here ASAP. Pick us up, we've got a rescue mission in Pearland."

"Already twirling the rotors Major. Tommy called me on the radio and told me you might be wanting a ride."

"Good man. See you in a few."

By the time he was done talking, the vehicles were ready to roll with a multitude of Army, Navy, and Marine volunteers; as well as some civilians tagging along in their personal trucks. William rode with them, so they could find the station. Most of them didn't know the area. Once the Chinook arrived, Bert, Rosa, and the five members of a Seal Team all jumped on. The pilot hit the gas hard, hoping to be fairly close behind the Cobra and Apache. Steve and Davis split between them. With the Humvee, large truck, and others having a five-minute head start the helicopters would still be there way ahead of them; Pearland being forty miles away.

Chapter 2

Approximately 4am

Pearland, TX.

"Damn. It's really dark out still. Switching to night vision. Maybe I can see someone running around down there." Major Pete "Dragon Rider" Hammond told Captain Thomas "Tommy Gun" Blair to do the same. Unfortunately, Gerry didn't have that option. Medical choppers hadn't felt the need for them, or they had disappeared during the initial overrun of zombies at the fire department where they found the bird.

"I've got no movement anywhere around the police station. You?"

Tommy circled again and said, "Nothing." The trucks with their troops were still a good ten minutes away.

"Hold on, I saw something. Switching to infrared." With a flick of a switch, he saw a bunch of fading red around the station but one really bright spot a block away in an alley. Whoever it was looked like they might be trying to hide behind a dumpster or something of the sort. Pete also saw a semi-large contingent of munchers two more blocks away going through trash cans and several others scattered around the area. The trucks might have to do some fighting when they arrived.

"This person doesn't look like a zombie. They're not moving as if they were scared of the helicopter but might be trying to stay out of the line of sight." Something pinged off the hull of the chopper. "What the hell!? This guy just shot at me." Several more bullets pinged and went flying by. The dumbass had tracer rounds in his gun. Easy to see where the fire was coming from. Frakkin' amateur.

"I want to light his ass up, but we don't know if he's friendly and doesn't know who we are, or if he was an attacker." Pete pulled back out of the line of fire and just watched over the red silhouette.

"Slow your roll, quick draw. Just keep tabs on him. Cavalry is almost here. Just a few more minutes till our ground backup arrives. then I'll unleash Vinny and the boys. They'll flush him out. One way or the other." Bert was very curious too. If he was an attacker, he wanted a word with him.

"If you insist, sir. I don't like taking potshots though."

Several minutes later, the Humvee came screaming around the last turn. Stopping a block away from the shooter, everyone got out and set up a firing line around the area for protection. The five members of the Seal Team roped down from the Chinook near the Humvee. With direction from Pete above, they got a good idea of where the man was. Warrant Officer Vincent Dupree signaled for his two primary shooters to move forward toward the end of the alley. He and another of his men would go around the other end and come up behind the person. His fifth man would head toward the police station with a few Marines to see what could be seen. Hopefully there were a few survivors, but it looked grim from their perspective. On coms, they coordinated their attack. Slowly they moved down each end of the block long alley. The guy must have heard something because he started shooting at Vinny's end. Then turned and fired some more down the other side.

"Back away. You're not taking me."

"My name is Warrant Officer Vincent Dupree. We are a United States Seal Team, sir. Please lay down your weapon so we can talk. We mean you no harm."

"Bullshit! You're here to kill me. My damn team left me behind. I ain't saying nothing." A few more shots Vinny's way before he paused. "Wait. Dupree? I know you!"

"You said your team left you behind? What team? And how do you know me?"

"You fucking got me booted five years ago. Fucking bastard."

Mulling that one over, Vinny suddenly remembered. "Kerrigan? Is that you? You're the only one I ever had to boot."

"Yeah, it's me, you dick. I had to go work for Ravenhearst because of you. I fucking loved being in the sandbox and you just had to bring me up on charges. Stupid fuck." He fired a couple more shots Vinny's way.

"Well, no shit I put you in the hurt. You fucking raped a woman."

"She was a Haji. Who fucking cared? But noooo. You had to jump on your high and mighty horse. You tried to get me thrown in the klink, you fuck."

"I would have put a bullet in your head if I was allowed." Over coms, he had his team moving up slowly behind whatever cover they could find the whole time. When Kerrigan fired a couple more rounds toward Vinny, E-5 Terrell Jackson moved around his last obstacle and put a bullet through the man's shooting shoulder.

"Owww! Goddamn, motherfucker!" Just as Terry came up to him, he tried to raise his rifle again. Terry kicked it out of his hands and hit him with a hell of a right cross. Kerrigan went down, spitting up blood and seeing stars. Most people would be out cold, but Kerrigan had a really large and thick head, so Terry hit him again as he tried to rise.

"Thank you, Terry. Let's get him over to the station and find out what happened."

As they arrived, his man came out the front door to talk. The door was no longer there. It was now lying on the inside floor with scorch marks along the hinges. A large irregular crevice now stood gaping. E-4 Jeremy "Germ" Turnball came out shaking his head. He had been listening to what had been going on in the alley but hadn't wanted to disturb his boss at the time.

"All dead sir. Five officers, three other men, two women, and…a kid sir. They killed a fucking child, sir. Maybe six years old." He took a second to catch his breath. "We also found a body wearing a Ravenhearst flak jacket and a blood trail leading out and around the back of the building. No body with the trail. Either he's running, a muncher, or zombie food somewhere." A tear formed in this hard man's eye. "A goddamn kid, sir."

"Take a few minutes and grab some water, Germ. I'm sorry you had to see that. Again. I'm going to see if I can get some answers from this piece of shit." He patted his man on the back.

"So, Kerrigan. What can you tell us? I was just informed of what you did to the police station and all those poor people. Innocent civilians and a little kid. Why?" Out of frustration he punched him across the jaw.

"Hehe. So what. They would have been zombie food anyway."

"Talk. Now."

"I ain't telling you shit."

"Well, because you were too cowardly to kill yourself, you like to flap your gums, and we found another body, we have confirmation you work for Ravenhearst. Your dumb ass is already talking to us. So spill the rest."

"Ravenhearst is running and gunning everywhere. They were prepared for this shit, man. They will have the whole nation wrapped up within a month. Our people are everywhere that matters. We're hitting wherever we can find guns. What better place than a police station? We're going after military depots next. You're fucked." He spit more blood out of his mouth and laughed with a red grin.

"That it?"

"You ain't getting nothing else out of me bitch." His smile was getting real irritating to Vinny.

"Well then. You're of no use to anybody then." Vinny pulled his gun and shot him in the head. "And you aren't doing nothing else ever again." He then spit on the corpse.

The helicopters all landed wherever they could find good enough spots and shut down. Bert jumped out and moved toward the station doorway. Walking through, he assessed how bad it was. Sadness was written all over his face as he saw each of the dead people that had put up one hell of a fight against extraordinary odds. Once past the bodies, he also noticed that every gun, bullet, grenade, piece of body armor, and any other material of weaponry that would prove useful was cleaned out. Completely. This was the true purpose of the kill zone he was walking through. Confirmed by Kerrigan. To kill all these innocent people just for more weaponry. Ravenhearst. Now near the top of his shit list. Right below zombies.

With that thought, he could hear a few shots ring out beyond the building.

"Are we okay out there?" Bert asked over the same com system the Seals used.

"Just a few unwelcome guests, sir. We've got this. It looks like Ravenhearst wiped out a boatload of Z's while taking down the station but the sound we've made has brought a few more." Vinny piped up as he put another round through a skull.

Rosa came up behind Bert and put her hand on his shoulder. She could see the pain on his face from viewing the carnage around him. So unnecessary. He walked over to the radio and saw that it was damaged. Needing to get a message out, he went back outside to the Humvee to use its dash radio.

"This is Major Bertram Bharata of the U.S. Navy. I am currently standing outside the Pearland Police station. Do not come here for help. Repeat. Do not come here for help. We have another enemy to battle for all those listening. The military contractor company Ravenhearst is not here to help you. I repeat. Do not trust Ravenhearst. They killed everyone here before we could arrive." He stopped talking for a few minutes for any response.

"This is Pervy Mervy in rural Pearland. Is there anywhere safe for those of us having a hard time?"

Bert took a minute to think and then said, "Yes sir. To anyone listening. If you can make it to Highway 288 and F.M. 518, we will stay in the area until noon. That gives you...seven hours. Wake everyone you know. Talk to anyone that will listen. Spread the word about Ravenhearst. I know I am just a voice on the radio, but I have a multitude of Army, Navy, and Marines backing me. We will be flying a Cobra, Apache, medical chopper, and Chinook over the area periodically. From one end of Pearland to the other. If anyone can't make it by noon or you don't have transportation, call on the radio or somehow flag us down. Everyone else bring as many vehicles as you can. We will need them."

"Major. We are pretty well set up here in Alvin. I don't have many officers left but a big bunch of civilians. We've raided everywhere we can and have plenty of munitions. The local high school was big enough and easily defensible. If anyone is closer to us and can get here, you are welcome."

"Thank you, sir. What is your name?"

"Sherriff Ingram. Twenty-one years on the force and ready to help however I can."

"I'll keep that in mind. I will try to get to you on my way back, sir. I think we should talk."

"You're welcome any time, my friend."

"Major? This is Perry in Rosharon. Can I get a pick up somehow? I'm stuck out here at my house in a wheelchair. I'm running out of food. Maybe a week left. Plenty of ammo though. I've only had to shoot three of those things."

"That must be nice. I wish I could say that myself."

"Well, sir, I'm in the middle of nowhere in a small house. No real reason for them to come by. Just caught a couple trying to get some wildlife a couple days ago. That's the only reason I've even seen them. Except on TV of course."

"Give me directions and we'll come and grab you." Bert wrote down everything and handed it to Gerry. He sent a couple Marines with Gerry just in case they had to shoot something. Gerry got up and gone as soon as the chopper was ready.

"One last thing before we move out people. If anyone can get down to Lake Jackson, please do. Some good people have control of the Super Wal-Mart down there and are trying to set up a longer-term solution in a neighborhood. For those that can hear me further away. If you can contact any military base, do so. Do so cautiously though.

I don't know which ones are compromised. Fort Hood is safe. I have been in contact with them. I have been unable to get ahold of anyone at Ellington or in Galveston yet. Tell them Bert sent you and ask for their commander, General Stephen Willoughby. He's a very good man and his people love his leadership. For what it's worth, I vouch for him." Bert took a drink of water. He was doing a lot of talking and his mouth was getting parched.

"We are also in control of the Naval Air Station in Corpus Christi. Along with the Army Depot and U.S. Coast Guard station there. That is where I am from. If anyone can hear me that might be nearer to Corpus, contact Captain Tonia Parnell of the Navy. She runs a tight ship there."

"Excuse me, Major. My name is Shirley in Katy. That is on the west side of Houston. Do we know of anything near me? I haven't eaten much in the last two days."

"So far, I don't. I'm sorry. We can come get you though."

"I've got this, Major. My name is John Parks. I am on the southwest side of Houston. We have a compound of warehouses that are completely secure. I also have a helicopter and plenty of fuel. Shirley, if you will switch to channel eighteen, I will be with you in a second. She will be safe. I promise that."

"Thank you, John. I need to meet with you too at some point. Maybe tonight if you can?"

"Yes sir. We have someone by the radio at all times. We have a few CBs set to different stations. Call whenever you're ready."

"Good. Thank you again." Once done, John switched channels and began talking to Shirley while Bert continued coordinating things.

Bert got most of his men moving towards the meeting point right then. He figured to be on the radio for a while, so he kept a squad of people with him till he was done. Vinny, Terry, and Rosa refused to leave his side while he worked the radio. They kept up a perimeter and Tommy Gun stayed overhead. Twenty minutes later Tommy called out.

"Guys. It's time to go or be ready to unleash a shitload of lead."

"How bad?"

"Let's just say the amount of noise we've made with the helos has brought out a multitude of party guests and you definitely don't have enough snacks and beer."

"Got it." Bert turned to see the others already moving toward the Chinook for takeoff. His pilot was already churning the air getting the bird up and running.

While they loaded up, they continued to listen in on all that was being said. With a smile on his face from the mass cooperation, they headed toward the highway to sit a spell. Once there, Bert was back on the radio again. Different frequencies this time so he could contact his own people and get informed of what they had found out about other bases and groups. Like John Parks, he had the different radios with them set to different channels. It was turning into a very good day. After such a gruesome and auspicious beginning.

Chapter 3

Near 11am

Highway 288 & F.M. 518

Gerry returned with their new passenger, Perry. The poor man had lost his legs in New York during that fateful day the towers fell. September 11th, 2001 had drastically turned his life upside down. Walking down the street, he had tried to help a few others when the first tower was hit. A couple of innocent bystanders were victims of debris and he was getting them to safety. The devastation was worsened by the second plane. Near one hundred minutes later the North tower fell and Perry Singer was partially crushed from the falling building. He was rescued about an hour later but the damage to his legs was too much.

Perry had been in New York to try and sell his Mechanical Engineering skills. He had been downsized when he lived in Dallas and figured why not try a job in the most architectural city in the nation. Bouncing from firm to firm for a week had put him in that horrific spot that day. The day some sick and worthless pieces of shits decided to strike innocent people in their endless and pointless Jihad against the greatest nation to have ever been. The man was a survivor and still being alive in Zombieville proved it.

"Welcome Mr. Singer. Glad to have you aboard." Bert walked over to him and made him feel at home with his new friends.

"Happy to be here, Major. I hope I can pull my own weight. So to speak."

"Well, let's start off with calling me Bert. We don't stand on military protocol now. Unless some of the men insist, that is. Right, Vinny?"

"Yes sir, Major, sir. As long as I am by your side, that's what you are to me."

"Oy. You're killing me."

"Well Bert. I still have skills that might help somewhere. I have a lot of engineering experience."

"Definitely something we need. Of course, what we might need will probably be below your skill set."

"Whatever and however I'm needed. I will do. Now. Where's the beer? I sure could use one."

"Vinny. Get this man a beer. Or whatever we have. And don't tell me we don't have one somewhere. Cuz if we don't, then something's wrong with you people and I need replacements." Laughing, he clapped Vinny on the shoulder and watched as he pushed Perry's chair toward the coolers.

Multiple vehicles had arrived with a hodgepodge of people over the last couple hours. They brought everything they could with them, including more animals. Their initial little group had turned into a gigantic convoy that would return to Lake Jackson. Pieces of many families had arrived. Almost all had lost at least one close member and endured till they could arrive here. To join a much bigger group. To rebuild. To grow and live on.

"Incoming helicopter." Tommy Gun had seen it on radar and called down ahead.

"What do we have, Tommy?" Bert was eager in hope but with a small amount of trepidation.

"Major Bharata. This is John Parks. May I approach and land?"

"Come on in, Mr. Parks." After landing on the north part of the highway, John stepped out along with two friends.

"Howdy do Major. I'm John. This is Peter and that is Jack. Good friends and fellow servicemen."

"Welcome John." He shook each of their hands. "Peter, Jack. I wasn't expecting you to come to me."

"Well, sir. I'm probably a lot like you. I wanted to see your group operate unexpectedly."

"True. True. That's why I wanted to come to you. Smart man."

"Well, sir. I was hoping that you and a few of your trusted men would come up anyway. I think you'll like what we've done. We have a big well, solar power, several warehouses, a couple helicopters, full fencing, etc. etc." John grinned. "Sorry. I sound like I'm trying to sell you on it."

"It sounds really good to me. You must have seen this coming." Vinny walked up and handed them each a beer. It seems that one of the vehicles brought to their little outing had been a Coors beer truck. Fully stocked. "Thank you, Vinny."

"Beer truck with running cooler. Heaven where you can find it, right?"

"Vinny, this is John, Peter, and Jack." Turning to the new guys, he said "men, this is my right hand. Warrant Officer Vincent DuPree. He is the commanding officer of our Seal team. Vinny is also dubbed my Secretary of Defense." The three of them looked at him funny. "I know, I know. They put me in charge and the title stuck from there. Don't fault me too much. We're trying to rebuild 'Murica here people." Bert said the last part in a President Bush accent with a smile.

"To each their own sir. No judgment here. And thanks for the beer. I'm more of a rum person but this goes down really well on a hot day. To your comment before. Yes, I saw something coming. I had already owned the warehouses and set up security for several years, but the solar power idea came a while back from my business partner. The well digging started the week before all of this. When Vancouver fell from the virus and then it moved into Washington state, I started preparing. My friends all came that could and we took in everyone that arrived. I turned no one away but everyone knew from the beginning that I was in control. I will not rule people, but I will also not endanger any of my friends or makeshift family. I guess you could say that I am a benevolent dictator of sorts."

"I understand. Your home, your rules. I must ask though. What did you do that you needed warehouses to yourself? If you don't mind my asking?"

"I…um." John debated for about five seconds. "Screw it. I wrote travel books and killed people."

cough Doing a spit take, Bert asked, "Say what?"

"I got rid of trash after I confirmed they deserved to die. Even did work for the CIA. I took out that football player in Canada that was raping women a few years ago. I've also saved Senator Fred Cruz from a vindictive bitch in Congress and some Ravenhearst kill squads. Oh. And he's at my compound too."

"Seriously. Shit, John. I'm intrigued. I have to meet the senator. I was really hoping for him to run for President next year. It would have been nice to have a man in the White House that thought like Ronald Reagan again. Been too long."

"More than happy to oblige. He's actually awaiting the outcome of this little meeting."

Thinking for a minute, Bert remembered something. "That player. I saw something about that back then. That poor woman wouldn't describe who saved her for nothing. Gave the cops absolutely nothing to go on." Contemplating it for a second, he now knew why. "She was protecting you. Good on her."

"That piece of shit was fixing to do it again when I arrived. I couldn't let it happen."

"Well, as you said before. No judgment. By the way John. Were you able to save that woman in Katy?"

"I talked to her and told her to get everything she had to have ready but pack light. I would be there in a couple hours. If you're up for that, we could go together." John took another big swig of his beer.

"I can do that. Give her a sense of comfort to meet us both."

"That's what I was thinking too."

"On that note, if you'll wait at least a while, we'll set off back your way."

"Sure. I think we could all use more beer anyway. I want to meet the rest of your Seals too. Just let me know when you're ready, Bert."

"Will do. And again, it's good to meet you."

Chapter 4

Just a Few Minutes Later

"Bert, we've got incoming again. Unfriendly, this time. A few infected scattered on the east and west. Easy-peasey. From the north is the problem. At least a hundred or so. They seem to be our first real force coming out of Houston." Michael Lawrence said. He had traveled from Lake Jackson with them.

"Tell Vinny please. I'm sure he will come up with something."

"He already knows and is gathering some heavy artillery. Just passing the intel."

"Good deal. Let me know if I can help."

Vinny conjured up something special with a little help from their birdy in the sky. It being Dragon Rider's turn in the air, he found some abandoned equipment and had let Vinny know earlier. Grabbing a few men, he had headed towards the south part of Beltway 8 that goes all the way around Houston. Still north of their position but out of range of the oncoming horde.

Dragon Rider hadn't informed them of what they would find, instead leaving it as a surprise. What was there made some of them giddy with excitement. Spreading out, they picked the small makeshift staging area clean. The National Guard had set up here when they were sealing off the city. It looked like they used the cross-traffic area of the Beltway and Hwy 288 as an easy source to close off this part of the city. Someone had been smart. Pushing all traffic to this one spot while closing off all the other exits.

"Dude. I have to drive it." Germ was freaking out.

"There's two. You can have one. If you can figure it out." Vinny was laughing his ass off at the way Germ was acting. In many ways, he was still young and goofy. In those that mattered, you wanted him watching your back.

"Woohoo!" Germ climbed up on the waiting tank and opened the hatch. Immediately, he fell off the side and all the way to the ground. "Fuck!" He bounced off the concrete in pain. "Owww!"

A shrieking and growling came from inside. A head popped out and snarled. The man was still in uniform with a scratched-up arm and small bite on the shoulder. He grappled his way out of the metal beast and started to jump off and after Germ. A shot rang out and the body went over the back side of the metal armament. Not quite down, the infected got up and scrambled after Germ again. A second loud boom came and put the man down for good. Five feet from Germ's feet.

"You okay?" Terry put his gun back in his holster and extended his hand.

"Fucking bastard whore mother pig fucking sum'bich. My shoulder hurts like a mother. I think I might have dislocated it."

"Let me see." Terry felt around the joint and moved his arm slightly. Germ screamed in pain. "Yep. Dislocated." He then yanked it outward without warning.

Screaming, he looked at Terry. "You big black bald motherfucker. That hurt."

"Yeah but you can move it now, can't you?" Terry was laughing as he walked away. "Say thank you."

Grumbling, Germ said, "Thank you." Quietly he said, "Motherfucker."

"I heard that buttmunch." Terry was still laughing because he knew Germ was actually grateful.

"If you two are done playing grab-ass, check the other tank before one of you climbs in and becomes lunch." Vinny had no desire to drive the monstrosity, so he was gathering whatever weapons and supplies he could.

After an hour of gathering and learning how to drive, they headed back to the rendezvous at F.M. 518. Germ and Jim Lee drove as fast as they could. Still the convoy went slowly back the five miles. They had set up the heavy weapons looking back toward Houston in case. They figured if any attack came it would be from there.

With Vinny's strategic thinking ahead, they were prepared for what was coming. It was just after midday and the sun was beating down hot. The smell coming from the swarm of feverheads was starting to overpower the joy of friendship and beer. Germ and Jim Lee hopped back through the hatches and got ready for action; each with another volunteer to load the cannons. The other three Seals got ready for what was left that might get through the initial fire. Several more personnel backed them up while many more volunteers took up a circular perimeter for the surrounding area. No chances were taken for any to slip through.

The infected had reached about the same spot they had picked up the tanks from. Not knowing how far they could shoot, Jim Lee fired first at what he thought might be the maximum trajectory. Falling way short at about two or more miles, he created a hole right in the middle of the freeway median. Knowing they were too far away, they sat and waited. Unhappily. This was the hardest part of combat for all warriors. The waiting. It didn't help that they were dying to start firing off a bunch of rounds. Mass destruction was a little boys wet dream and that's what they still were. Little boys in big badass bodies.

The hundred had gathered into almost two hundred by the time the horde was within range. Fifteen minutes later, they believed that the spacing was about right to start shelling. Germ was the next to fire. His shell fell at the tail end of the gigantic mob. Seems his cannon fired just a slight bit further. Jim Lee let loose at the same distance as before. His shot landed right in the middle of the pack. Bodies flew everywhere. Pieces of infected rained down for half a minute. Several stopped and fed on the remains while the many moved on. The tanks firing had a second effect of keeping the infected coming their way from the new sounds.

Germ and Jim Lee kept raining shells. The two navy volunteers inside were reloading as fast as they had learned in the little time they had. As soon as they would say 'loaded', the next shell would be off toward mass death. They both adjusted their aim down a little at a time between shells while each impact would send many more to instant afterlife. Some would stay alive for a few minutes and continue trying to crawl or drag themselves by hand toward Bert and the others. Then suddenly stop and either get trampled underfoot, die, or become food. Having no intellect or brainpower left didn't stop them from the pursuit of meat. They just kept coming until their bodies gave up mortality.

Once what was left of the horde were within a half a mile, the large armaments were useless. It was too easy for a shell to fly over their heads and be wasted so the Humvees got into position to fire the .50 caliber guns. Terry and a few others fired rounds from their M-203 grenade launchers into the crowd, causing more destruction. By the time the M-2 guns opened up, there was only twenty-five to fifty left. The Marines opened up and took out every other zombie heading their direction. Several more were still munching on the fallen here and there. Sniper shots from several people with rifles took them out one by one.

Not hearing from any others on the radio for help, they gathered up to head back towards Lake Jackson. It took a while for everyone to repack up, those without to find rides, and them all to make sure they were reloaded and ready for whatever may come. The tanks were an issue though. No use trying to drive them all the way back. Giant waste of fuel. Perry piped up for that though.

"Since y'all wiped out the crowd, take a run up the road a bit. About two miles up are a couple big truck stops. Bet there has to be at least one big rig up there. And there is a heavy hauler yard another mile down. Don't remember the name of the company but I guarantee there are some rigs waiting to be absconded with."

"Damn, Perry. That's a hell of an idea." Vinny grabbed a radio on one of the Humvees. It had a built-in loudspeaker to use. "I need a few volunteers. Anyone that can drive big trucks. We need at least two to help us liberate some rigs for hauling the tanks. I anticipate needing more later. So, if I can get about three or four of you, that would work."

Several actually came forward and volunteered. Might as well bring back as many trucks as possible and store them near the Wal-Mart. Now they could get a few with closed-in trailers on top of those needed flatbeds. It would make things easier when 'shopping' around for more supplies. Taking along a forklift each time as a just in case for bigger loads. 'Yeah' thought Vinny. This could work out great in the future.

"There's a big bulldozer back towards town. Construction site for a new shopping center.

Maybe there's more than one to move all the bodies out of the way. Otherwise, the road will be a pain in the ass to drive on. Too many pieces of muncher everywhere." Perry pointed back a few blocks to where the machinery could barely be seen.

"Hell to the yeah. I got that one. Anyone else wanna come see what they got?" Gerry had driven a few back hoes and the like over the years. He had a really nice back acre he had improved some time ago. Building a pond and so forth. A few people piped up and they all started towards the equipment.

The aircraft all lifted off before they went for the trucks. Bert and the others had things to do. The Apache and Cobra would follow Bert, Rosalita, Michael, William, and the Seals in the Chinook. Each of them would be behind John Parks and head towards the lady in need waiting in Katy. Gerry and Michelle would head back to LJ carrying Perry and his wheelchair once the dozing was done. It took a few more hours to get the tractor-trailer rigs and then load up the M1s. No one had ever put a tank on a flatbed before. It was challenging, and Jim Lee almost went over the side of his truck bed. That would have been such a waste. How the hell would they get it back upright if that had happened? Once they were tied down and the tracks chocked, the convoy got underway with Gerry flying overwatch.

"Captain Brink, this is Chief Grace. Come in."

"Go for Brink."

"Sir. We are seeing increased traffic along the shoreline leading down to the border. Believe to be cartel or the like."

"Got it. Increase air patrols. Arm them to the teeth. I'll head your way in the next few minutes." Captain Brink set the radio down with a small amount of unhappiness. He was really hoping to have longer getting to know these people. Oh well. Duty calls.

"Captain Brink to Major Bharata. Come in."

Muttonchop took the call and keyed up the interior mike. "Sir, got a call from Brink for you."

"Patch it through."

"Go for Bert."

"Sir, I've got to head back now. We've got some southern intruders on the coast. Could be hazardous for their health."

"All right. Sad to see you go so soon but we need to keep the coasts safe."

"Me too." A second passed and then he was back. "Looks like Colonel Garber is going back with me too. Maybe we can grab a couple volunteers, so we have transport. Otherwise, it will be a looong walk."

"All right. Let me know if you need help. I expect we're heading back tomorrow too."

"Good luck Major. Over and out."

The trip to pick Shirley up was uneventful and only took about thirty minutes to return to the warehouses from the time they got there. John had radioed ahead to Sheila Dobson, longtime friend, partner, and life manager, to make room for the four helicopters. Once they arrived a couple had to land on the far end of the compound. Peter and Jack took a Suburban over to the Apache and Cobra to pick up the pilots and returned. When everyone was at the main warehouse, John began his introductions. The first person to greet them was Sheila.

"Welcome to each of you. I'm Sheila Dobson, caretaker of John's assets. I mean that in the serious sense. Not the sexual. This is his lady Terry Vaughn. Can I get y'all something to drink?" Each of them shook their heads no except the pilots. They just wanted some water after being in the cockpits for a while. Out walked Senator Fred Cruz and his wife Lydia with smiles on their faces.

"Hello there. I'm Fred and this is my wife, Lydia." They shook each hand available and welcomed them.

"I know who you are Senator Cruz. You're a welcome sight. My name is Bertram Bharata. Call me Bert." He introduced each of those with him.

"I've come to understand that you are a Major in the Navy. And you have a pretty decent size group?"

"Yes sir. I'm Reserve, er…well I guess now I'm just another man helping out. Actually, a surgeon that just happened to be put in charge. Somehow. I'm not standing on any military protocol with anyone though. Too many civilians and I don't know how to lead really."

"Bullshit. You're a born leader Bert. That's why everyone elected you." Rosalita bumped Bert in the arm. "He's the reason so many are alive, sir. Hello. I'm Rosa. It's is a pleasure to meet you both."

"Delighted young lady. My eyes might be deceptive but are you two an item?"

"Are now. We worked together at the hospital but never went out before. Pickings are a little slim nowadays so…" She smiled as she said this.

"Hey! I resemble that remark. That actually stung a little." Bert acted offended.

"He's such a whiner sometimes."

Sheila came back with a couple water bottles for the pilots. John decided that it was time to introduce them to everyone else. They moved the group inside and gave quick and short highlights to everyone about what they witnessed and who the new people were. About an hour later, after all the questions were hurled at them and they asked their own, John gave a tour of the warehouse compound. He was delighted to show what his little survivor camp had accomplished. Both before and after the fall of humanity. It took a few more hours of walking and talking but an exchange of multiple ideas occurred during the walkabout. Bert was able to come away with a couple things that could help his and future groups too. When geeks get together, brain power is always enhanced, and the outcome can be magnificent.

Chapter 5

Late Evening

"Hey Bert. If you don't mind, I would like us to swing over Alvin please. My brother-in-law runs an RV park there and we haven't heard from him since the beginning." Michael was speaking into the headset, trying to be heard over the rotors. They had left after a few hours with their own things to do.

"Damn. I'm sorry to hear that. We've got time. I wanted to meet the officer in Alvin anyway. Let's do it." He keyed to the pilot. "Hey Muttonchop. Swing towards Alvin. Hold on. I don't know where it is either. I'll let Michael tell you." He keyed back over to Michael and had him guide the pilot. Lieutenant Elvis 'Muttonchop' Bennett listened intently and sped them through the sky.

Being a quick flight from southwest Houston, they were hovering over the park pretty soon. What they saw made Michael's heart drop. The fences had been overrun in a couple different spots and some bodies were scattered here and there. A pickup had run into one of the propane tanks while trying to get out and caused several fires from the explosion that had occurred. Several trailers were now burned out husks of their former selves. Doors were wide open or just plain hanging off a hinge. A couple of the infected poked out from the sound of the whirly birds. Hovering over Charles and Angelica's trailer, they opened the door of the Chinook and drilled the few zombies with some well-aimed shots.

Just in case, the Seals made their way down first and secured the area. The chopper landed but didn't wind down. 'Mutt' wanted to be ready for a quick extraction if needed. Pete and Tommy hovered overhead as security and to watch for more. Michael popped out and went to their front door. Amazingly, nothing seemed to be wrong with their particular house. He knocked. Feeling kind of stupid after he did it because the sound would have brought them to the door already. Just before he opened it, Terry stopped him.

"Let me go first. You never know, right?"

"Good idea. All I have is my 9mm on me."

Terry opened it and stood back, ready to fire with his Colt M4A1 assault rifle. Nothing. He moved into the house and scanned each room. No one was home. That was a good thing, Michael guessed. It seemed to be a good sign that they weren't infected and sticking around. He moved in after Terry cleared it. Looking around, Michael found no indication of where they may have gone. He mused as he went through Charles's room. He had a few paintings of comic characters like *Deadpool* killing zombies and some signed *Walking Dead* comics from the cast. There was even a full sized cardboard standup of Illidan from *World of Warcraft*. Just another fellow geek that had to leave precious cargo behind.

Michael only took about fifteen minutes to look through everything. No hot food or cold drinks indicated that it may have been a while ago when they left for greener pastures. Damn. He just realized something. Charles and Angelica's computer rigs were still standing, right where they always were. They must have left in a hurry. No way would a computer geek like Charles leave his baby behind. Even if he went to a shelter from a hurricane, he would have taken his computer. Seeing this really cemented the fact that Michael might never see them again. They left in a hurry.

"Hey Terry. Can you help me? I don't want to leave all of this behind. Charles may not be able to come back but I'm hoping we find him one day. He has some pretty cool stuff that should survive with us. It would be a waste to not grab it."

"What am I grabbing?"

"Those paintings and the framed comics on the wall. I'm going to snag the few boxes of comics and maybe a couple of his Batman statues and the like."

"I never got into comics, but I get your mindset. Some things need to be preserved." On his first trip through the front door he yelled at Germ to help them. Better to do this quickly than possibly get overrun while loading. Once Jim Lee and Papa got a hint of what they were bringing, they giddily ran inside to help. This was nerd-vana for them. Being Seals, they really didn't have the space to keep stuff like this before. Living from mission to mission most times and not having a real home, just apartments. They were more than happy to be the caretakers until Charles could come back and claim it. It only took them a few minutes to grab everything, including the computer rigs. Waste not, want not. When they all loaded back up, Mutt got them in the air. Once they were at flight height, they could see more Z's running their direction. Good timing for them to move.

The sad part that none of them knew was how close they had been to Charles and Angelica. The third day of the apocalypse, their defenses had been broken through. Charles had been trying to hold them back with the hundred or so bullets he had for his .45. This helped some of his residents get out since most had been hooked up to their vehicles ahead of time. Others just couldn't get lucky enough to even make it into their trucks.

Charles watched in horror as the nicest old lady he had ever known had been attacked from behind while trying to climb into her van. The feverhead had run flat out and leaped over a wheelbarrow and onto her back. Her husband got out and ran around to help but it was too late. Before he even reached her, another muncher jumped on him, tumbling him into the front fender. All Charles could do was shoot them in the head to ease their pain and then took out the zombies. Knowing he would lose, he had Angelica retreat into the house. She had been reloading the few magazines he had to help him.

They packed whatever food and water they could into backpacks. Being older, they were limited in the weight capacity but took whatever they could carry. Running would be hard but a fast walk was still better than inviting their guests in for dinner. Peeking out the back windows, seeing no zombies between them and their private gate, they snuck out. They spent the next hour putting as much room between them and the RV Park as possible. They were hoping to make it to the police station. Praying for help.

Unfortunately, infected were pretty active and out looking for food. They parked themselves in an empty home for a couple days. This was their life for about a week. Moving and stopping, bobbing and weaving. A little closer to the Alvin Police Department at a time. He kicked himself for neither one of them remembering their cell phones. His sister, Ann, must be worried sick. Not to mention his mom, Kay. These are the things he would dwell on when stopped for a night. Boredom was no joke and they really regretted having to leave so quickly without any fun things to do. It really did make Charles choke up knowing he would never get to see his expensive computer setup again. He may have just been a RV Park manager, but he enjoyed a little lite hacking, some programming fun, plenty of gaming, along with buying and selling comics on eBay.

The worst part was that they heard the helicopters go overhead. Both times. But how could they get them to notice that they needed help when so many infected swarmed the area. Any noise would have attracted them to their presence. Such was their lot in life at this time. The only thing they could do was to continue trying to get to help. One day at a time.

Chapter 6

Alvin, TX.

As the air crew approached Alvin, they radioed down to Sheriff Ingram of their arrival. It was getting late in the afternoon, but Bert wanted to make sure to meet this new group too. Better to use the trip you're already on than waste fuel on a needless second one. The plan was not to stay too long, and fuel was running down toward the low side. Tommy Gun and Dragon Rider both circled the area, but further out, so they didn't bring the infected right to the high school. That would be bad.

As he stepped off the helicopter, the Sheriff came out of the rooftop door to greet him. They shook hands but didn't say anything till they got back downstairs. Kind of hard to talk with the earsplitting sounds of rotor wash beating down on them. After Muttonchop and the Chinook dropped Bert off on the roof, he shut down but kept it prepped for takeoff.

"Good to meet you sir. How are things in your neck of the woods?" Bert pumped the Sheriff's hand with a smile.

"We're holding up pretty good. Bert, is it? Call me Billy. I have about a hundred plus civilians and half a dozen of my own officers." You could see the sadness behind his words.

"I imagine you lost more than you could save though. Almost everyone I worked with is gone, too."

"We did pretty well considering how fast it all went wrong down here. A lot of my officers were lost trying to help others on that first day. Just about all of the EMTs and firefighters went down too. It started with a major pileup near Highway 35. There is a major signal light near the Wal-Mart that produces a bunch of traffic. The accident ate up most of our resources that day. Unfortunately, no one knew what awaited them. I happened to be off, so I guess I got lucky. One of those in the accident was infected. It just snowballed from there. I don't know if it was a man or woman but it bit or whatever enough people to cause a catastrophe. My officers tried to keep working, even after being bitten. Many of those ended up at the hospital before they changed, and my town was done from there. All of this is second hand knowledge. One of my guys made it back to the department before succumbing. My second-in-command had to take him down." As they were talking, they had been walking towards the rest of the group.

"Sad state of affairs sir. I see I'm attracting a crowd."

"Everyone! This is Major Bertram Bharata. He is part of a rather large group. Welcome him. But do it quickly please. He has places to be. Saving the world and all that." After a second, he couldn't help but laugh. It had been a while since he could joke like that.

"Maybe just a small part of it but I appreciate the boost to my ego." He went around shaking the hands of those that came up to him. Bert spoke to as many as possible in the next thirty minutes and then sat down with Sheriff Ingram for a little while longer.

Billy had the same ideas Bert had once they had gotten established. Run out and scavenge everything they could. Unlike Bert though, they hadn't made long-term plans. There was nowhere to plant or grow things in the immediate vicinity. They talked about exchanging goods and services as needed. Billy figured that they needed to branch out to the countryside to put down some roots for the future. Keeping in touch via radio, Bert was going to help them establish a way to produce electricity and whatever else they needed help for. Manpower was becoming plentiful as they grew. People just had to be willing to roam around to new places.

After about an hour stay, it was time to leave. Bert wanted everyone to be back at base in Wal-Mart by dark. No use being out at night if you didn't need to be. They radioed up to Muttonchop and walked up to the roof. Shaking hands again, Bert jumped on and off the three choppers went.

Arriving near sunset, the neighborhood was a bevy of activity. Even though the Pearland trip had been a busy one, it looked as if those left behind had actually done much more work. Albeit heavy labor. They were almost done cordoning off another whole two blocks for more people to call home. The massive amount of labor had been the shot in the arm that Michael, William, and the others had needed. The big group that came down a couple hours ago didn't hurt either. As soon as the new influx of men and women arrived from Pearland, many of them jumped out and helped secure the area immediately. They let their wives, girlfriends, and children unpack and unload everything while many men and several more women proceeded to help with the fencing in. It was really starting to look more like a mini-fortress type setup.

Once they arrived back in Lake Jackson, Michael found his wife. Giving her what little information he had acquired, she teared up with not knowing about her brother. She hugged him hard. After a minute or three, she collected herself. Ann was strong. She had to be, and she knew it. Her family needed her to be. Wiping her tears away, she kissed Michael and went to help with dinner. Michael watched her go. His boys were busy elsewhere, but he figured Ann would tell them later anyway. Steve Hull and Davis Masters walked up to Michael with a sense of urgency.

"Dude. We found a goldmine at the Target store once we finally got back. Had to kill a few more munchers but it was worth it. Wouldn't have given them any money during civilized times. You know. Because of that whole letting men into women's restroom shit but it was pretty ready to be plucked. Like a twenty-pound turkey for Thanksgiving. Guess no one else still human wanted to go in there either." He chuckled a little. Steve was never one to hold back. Had something to do with his Marine Corp training and long length of time served. Or it was just a personality trait. Whatever.

"Yeah. Even snagged a bunch more Playstations and X-Boxes. Amazing how zombies don't care to play video games anymore. There were a great many Nintendo packs too. Grabbed as much Mario stuff as we could. Most of those games wouldn't need internet when it goes down, so that will help the kids. Our guys had picked it clean of food stuffs before; their priorities were different from ours. We didn't have a lot of time. One of the mother's asked us to try and find some board games and the like so out we went; knowing you would be a while. Unfortunately, that's not the only news." Davis took a breath before unleashing the bad part. "We saw more evidence of them bunching up. Driving through the neighborhoods earlier, there were several groups of them here and there. The weirder part was how many of them are just standing around. A few even ran away from us. That's a first."

"Bert told us about them last night. I guess y'all weren't in that conversation. It seems there are many different personalities, even in the infected. We're gonna all talk tonight in a kind of town hall type meeting. That guy out of Houston, John Parks, has a compound full of people. They have one hell of a setup. We learned some things that can help us in sustainability. That man is gonna be a hell of an ally as we rebuild. Wait till I tell you about him and his buddies. Oh. And

Senator Fred Cruz is with him. They've been friends for years, come to find out. This apocalypse is getting interesting, to say the least."

"Well, all right. Enough chit-chatting. I'm dying for some food. I don't I've had anything but jerky and beer since we left this morning." Davis nodded in the affirmative. "Do you think your wife will care if I snag a biscuit while she's not looking?"

"I think she'll kick your ass if you don't at least ask." Davis's wife, Danielle, had been helping a lot with the cooking.

"Well, if she ain't there, what she doesn't see wont' hurt me." All three of them laughed. "Well. It's worth a shot. All right guys, I'm off. I think tomorrow is going to be fun." Steve clapped Michael on the shoulder and they all walked off together.

"Hey Bert. How do you like our version of Woodbury? Everyone is feeling much more secure." Steve found him after their talk with Michael. They watched as some of the new recruits worked on the fencing. Plywood was moving off the piles as quick as they could nail it in place.

"God no. Not that town. How about we go with Alexandria instead? At least that one didn't have as much of a despot undertone."

"You're probably more of the *Walking Dead*-head than me. I tried watching but never could get caught up. I'm still stuck near the end of season four."

"Well, you should have time to catch up when things settle down again. Whenever that might be." Bert then asked him to get all the higher ups of the group together. Michael had come up next to them by this time and nodded okay to Steve.

"Sorry about that Michael. This is your group. They look to you, not me. I overstepped."

"Not at all, Bert. I also think it's good for us to meet like this. Inform everyone we can together instead of word of mouth. But like you said. They, for some reason, look to me right now. That might change as they get to know y'all more." Michael and Bert walked along towards the middle of the original block they had secured the night before. This seemed to be the impromptu gathering spot for now.

"I think they will always look to you first. Kind of like having your first girlfriend. You never give her up if possible."

"While everyone is gathering, I'm going to call Wally's and my boys. I need to get a bead on where the hell my kids are. They've become quite independent already and it scares the shit out of me." Michael walked off towards one of the Humvees.

"See you in a few." Bert turned and saw that Rosalita was right there with him again. She was quickly becoming his pseudo-bodyguard and very quiet sidekick. He didn't even realize she was there. Sneaky.

"Hey Rosa. You're pretty good at this stealth thing. I didn't know you popped up."

"Been here a while. Listening. I'm trying to stay out of your highness's way. My liege." She came closer and gave him a peck on the cheek.

"Very funny. I'm no one's king. Don't want to be. Just want to do whatever I can to help us survive."

"Doin' great, babe. I think you've got some competition though. Senator Cruz will probably run the show eventually."

"God, I hope so. I'm flying by the seat of my pants with all of this. I just hope all the others we pick up agree. He's a good man." Bert grabbed her hand and they walked on.

"Aaron. What are y'all up to? I haven't gotten to see you in a while." Michael spoke with a small amount of worry in his voice.

"Hey dad. Just running around collecting up some stuff for Danny. He's been talking to the engineer in Corpus off and on today. Trying to put Danny's skills to the test. While everyone else is building up the neighborhood, we're working on a long-term solution to what soon should be an electrical crisis. Being close to the STP (South Texas Project) nuclear plant should give us more time than most but the grid will shut down eventually."

"Good thinking. Is there anything we can help with?"

"Not yet. We're discussing a trip to the plants later. Taking three trucks. We found some trailers for hauling at the Tractor Supply. We figure to grab whatever engineering books we can find along with as much equipment as we can load. Anything and everything might be useful one day."

"Okay. I'll leave you to it. Don't get bit. Your mother would kill me." Michael chuckled.

"Please dad. We have some makeshift body armor, too. Baseball, hockey, and police riot gear. Bring them on."

"All right then. Are ya'll coming back soon?"

"Not for another hour or so. I've got Danny, Jose, Kylar, and of course Wayne with me. We're loading up some stuff from the two local satellite television depots. Some of the stuff we need for power. Once we're loaded, we'll head your way."

"I won't even ask what or how. At least someone knows something. Well, we're fixing to have a big sit down with Bert and the new people. See you in a while for dinner. Love you boys. Be careful."

"Will do dad. We might have girlfriends to come back to." A smile could be heard in Aaron's voice.

"I won't ask but you will tell later. Got it?"

"Yes, sir."

"Bye, son."

"In a while dad."

Michael phoned over to the Wal-Mart next. "Warren. How goes things?"

"Making real good progress here. Almost done making the fencing bigger and less see-through. There's plenty of room out back for the animals but they do make a lot of noise. We can sustain them here for a long time as long as we can continue to get hay and feed. At some point, we'll need a much larger area for the sheep and horses to graze naturally."

"Okay. Hopefully we can find another farm or ranch to move to. Or maybe we'll just have to take everything to the prison. Plenty of room there." Michael was trying to form options in his head. "Do you need more manpower tomorrow? Or anything?"

"No, we should be done here by tomorrow afternoon. We're in the process of building a few guard towers around the perimeter. Still get some stragglers because of the bleeting, neighing, and barking. Guys on the roof can't catch everything. They've got enough on their hands watching over the front and further out. Right now, some of the guys are out front trying to maneuver the tanks in the parking lot. We're starting to run out of room out front. At least when we have friends over. I still can't believe we have them. I hope to see them in action one day." He paused for a second. "Actually. I wish we didn't have to." Warren was directing one of the volunteers while talking.

"I understand. It was an awesome sight to witness but it is also a tragedy to have to be a part of."

"Well, hey. They just came back inside. Quickly too. I can hear a few shots, so I guess all the noise brought some of the infected along. Let me go check on everything."

"Sure. But Warren. Can you make it over here for a get-together with Bert?"

"Yes. Give me half an hour."

"Good. I think Bert and the rest plan on leaving tomorrow morning."

"Be there soon."

"Dad said he loooves you." Aaron teased Wayne.

"Shut up, Aaron. I guarantee he said he loves you too. Dumbass. Get over here and do something." Wayne was helping Kylar lug a big load of cable to the truck.

"Pfft. What else do we need from here?"

"Danny and Jose are gathering some dish stuff. I don't know what else. Help them."

"Yessir, master sir." They spent the next thirty minutes or so gathering whatever Danny said to. He had the list.

"We got company!" Wayne hollered. Not a second or two later a shot rang out. Then a few more. They all dropped whatever was in their hands and ran to the front door. About a dozen munchers were quickly heading their way. They had no way of knowing if the small amount of noise they made or just their scent gave them away but who cared. Time to kill them all. Each took a small segment of the group and just started firing. A couple of good headshots but mostly torso hits. One just kept coming. Shot twice in the chest, the Z was on a mission. Nothing but food on its mind. The man's melon exploded two steps away from Wayne. Aaron had taken one last shot. Kind of couldn't miss from that distance.

"Gnarly! Kind of like spoiled fruit juice everywhere." Kylar was admiring Aaron's handiwork.

"Let's get this done before more show up." Aaron had become the leader whenever they were out on their own, with Danny guiding their hands to pick up what they needed. They finished up without another incident and headed back towards the Hastings to pick up the men's girlfriends. Couldn't go to dinner without grabbing the ladies. They would kill them and then cut them off from any sex they hoped to have.

Chapter 7

Lake Jackson

Just Before Dinner Time

The gathering was quite large by the time Bert and the others were ready to speak. The majority was all there. The core group consisting of William, Michael, and fellow operators from the plant along with those Bert brought over and the huge number of new friends from the Pearland area. Warden Perryman from the Clemens Unit prison farm even took time to come and meet everyone. He had come to give his own updated situation. Right now, their primary source of beef and vegetables were the farm.

"Ladies and gentlemen! Let's kick this pig." A smattering of laughter occurred. Some of the older folks remembered that movie where Kelsey Grammer was talking about starting up the old World War II submarine in *Down Periscope*.

"A few people will give updates over the next--however long it takes. I want to begin by giving my thanks to all of you. We have all come from different walks of life but are giving our all to rebuild. We have run into some that want us to fall already. Well, not really us but they seem to want to rule over all or at least do whatever they want. Ravenhearst. Know that name people. Remember it." Bert paused for a few seconds.

Continuing, he said, "I'm not sure how many of you have ever heard of them. Those of us that have served in the last twenty years certainly have. We've seen how these military contractors operate. They don't care who gets hurt and didn't have much government oversight before the fall. Now. Well. Now, no one is watching them. Unless there's someone they answer to. Who knows?" Pausing again, he choked back a small amount of bile at what he had to say next.

"Ravenhearst killed several people in Pearland. All for some weapons and ammo. A child was taken for no reason. Along with some civilians and civil servants. This cannot stand. If we encounter them, be cautious. There may be a few good ones but that has not been my experience so far. No one should go out alone. Period. I am not in charge but that is my suggestion. I will now relinquish the podium, or table as it is. I will give a little more information at the end. Michael?"

Standing, Michael took the head of the large table. There wasn't really any other way to address everyone, so they made do. Around the table was everyone that ran the Lake Jackson group and Bert's contingent. They were trying to speak as loud as possible for as many that could to hear. They didn't want to use any kind of PA system for fear of bringing too many uninvited guests. As it was, they could hear the occasional suppressed sound coming from either end of the street. These shots were their security taking down the few munchers that came to visit.

"Good people. Who have traveled from villages near and far. Lend me your ears." A few instinctively acted like they were taking off their ears and threw them onto the stage in jest. "That's disgusting." Michael said this last in a fake British accent. Those same people just started laughing while all the others just stared at them. Some of those that got it whispered the joke to others.

"What the hell is this? Quote your favorite movie night." Steve Hull, former Marine Force Recon, roared out. "For those of you not old enough to remember it, that was Cary Elwes from *Robin Hood: Men in Tights*. A classic from Mel Brooks. Some of you youngins could learn some good old-fashioned humor from that great man. Sorry people. You're being led by a bunch of geeks. God help us all."

"Yeah, yeah. Back to business." Michael's wife was just holding her head in fake shame. Ann had always known what a goofball he was.

"As you can see, progress is going great here. The guys have really been doing a wonderful job trying to clear and build up enough space for us to live in a small amount of peace. A few people are still working right now to finish the wall around the third block. This will give us all enough room to sleep in beds or on couches for tonight. We still need at least two more blocks to have space for everyone to have their own beds. We're growing fast people. That's a good thing. I hope that others around the country are too, but we just don't know right now. There is still much to discuss but it needn't be done right now. This is all I have for y'all so I'll give Warren the soapbox now. Thank you." Michael shook hands with Warren and sat down.

"Yay. My turn. This will be short. Right now, I am overseeing Wal-Mart operations. Really not as big time business-like as it sounds. This is our staging area for the helicopters when here and the animals not at the prison. We are rotating shifts of watch on the rooftop and they should be finished with the guard towers in the animal pen soon. If not already. I was telling Michael this earlier, but you should all know. We need to find a more permanent solution for the few animals we have because I also think we need to breed as many of the food producing ones as possible. This will require land and more fencing." Warren took a sip of water and then continued.

"We have several months of grain, feed, and hay available for now. It's not urgent. But don't get complacent either. If you find something worthy of checking out while you scavenge, bring it to our attention. Maybe we can start fortifying it now before things run out. We still get our own straggling zombie types, but bullets are plentiful for now. With that, I suggest we start looking for ways to produce more. Eventually, we will have to reload the shells. I'm hoping several of you good ole country boys know how cuz I sure don't. One last thing. Wal-Mart still has plenty of food and snacks. If you need blankets, pillows, bedding, or whatever you can't find in the houses, just let me know. I'm pretty sure we got it. Target is also ripe for the picking and we haven't even begun to explore the parts of the mall not destroyed by the plane. And as a reminder, don't forget your teeth. We got toothpaste and mouthwash too. No one needs mouth problems right now. I think that's the one thing we don't have so far. A dentist. That's all I have for you. Feel free to grab me after the meeting if you need something. We'll try to accommodate. Oh. On that note. I sure could use someone willing to be my secretary. I'm having a hard time keeping up with stuff and my wife is really busy feeding everyone. And yes. You can be a man. I don't discriminate." Once the laughter died out, Warren stepped down while Danny took the spotlight next.

"Howdy do all. Your local Hastings squad has been hard at work too. I've been talking to Peter Stormare in Corpus. Peter has a doctorate in mechanical engineering and was working on a second in electrical when Zombie hell hit. Through his knowledge, we have been collecting items needed to create our own independent power. We all know the grids will go down sometime soon. I'm nowhere near ready yet, so don't get too happy. It's going to take a while to get all the supplies to set up." Danny held up his hands as a great many groans came from the crowd. They understood but were hoping for miracles.

"Hold on. Hold on. I have some good news to go with the bad. We have another option. Mechanical usage of a sort. This idea will only take a couple days at the most. One of the quickest ways is by bike. We set up multiple bicycles on stands, take the tires off the back, and hook belts around the rims and to a motor. These belts will drive a motor at the other end. From here we will hook cables from the motor to batteries and then to power inverters. Voila. Electricity. Now, this is small scale obviously. But. It is the quickest fix. If we can find a great many batteries, we can store up energy before the nuclear power stops. We believe this is the best and easiest option for now. If someone comes up with other ideas, please share. I know there has to be other ways. So. Everyone that goes out from now on, please collect bicycles and batteries. If you see large automobile type belts and wires that you think might work, bring them too. You can never have too much material."

"We left a bunch of bikes at Academy. They were useless at the time. And Wal-mart should have a bunch more." Alberto Lopez, Michael's best friend spoke up. He and Davis had wiped out Academy the first week of everything that was useful at the time. Or so they thought at the time.

"Good idea. Can you hit them up tomorrow? We could get started soon. Maybe someone else can get batteries from Autozone and O'Reilly?" Danny was smiling because others were suddenly seeing this come together.

"My tire and lube area at Wal-Mart was recently stocked with batteries. And you might find some of the wiring you need there. Don't get the ones in the bay area though. Those are returns with problems." The small voice that rang out came from Nina Boldin. She had been the auto manager a week ago.

"Excellent. So, for the rest of my bad news. Not really. Just an update. Solar power will be our long-term solution, but it will take a lot of panels and storage to supply the growing neighborhood. This is why it will take so long. We have a bunch of materials to collect and then try to put together. It will be trial and error for a while since none of us has ever done this before. I plan on making copies of the shopping list and dispersing them to everyone that goes out. Don't go out of your way though. Food and supplies still come first. We can live without electricity. We can't live without sustenance. That's it for me. The long and the short of it. Thank you all for your patience." Danny moved away and sat down for a long-awaited beer. His girlfriend, Rachel, kissed him on the cheek once he was sat.

"Good evening everyone." Warden Anthony Perryman was next. Almost none of the people had met him. This was his first trip away from the prison.

"My name is Anthony Perryman. I am the warden at the Clemens Unit on Highway 36. Just an FYI, I have no violent criminals left so please feel safe in that knowledge. I had a few of my more—zealous guards kill all of those before they abandoned their jobs. Not by my word though. They just did it. What I have left are about one hundred ex-inmates of the much lesser infraction type. They are doing good and being quite helpful in this new world. I also have five guards left. My best men that didn't let me down. Their families are there too." He bowed his head for a second. "Well, most of their families. Like everyone else, they lost people too."

The warden took a minute to recover. "Fencing is going well there too. If possible, we could use a lot more manpower though. We have a great many acres to try and cover for all the horses and cattle. The farms are thriving but that was already underway before the zombies hit. In the future, we will have to find other ways to turn the ground and plant. We all know that fuel will run out one day. That's a problem for next year. We have a boatload for now. I suggest finding some fuel rigs, Michael. That could help you too on long runs later. Mr. Ritter and his friends have been able to teach my boys much. We've had a LOT of visitors in the last week. To combat that, we have a dozen horsemen riding the perimeter at any point in time. Every worker walks around strapped too. Only two have gotten by the riders so far and we lost a horse. Those rolling the farm equipment have a secondary shooter with them at all times now. This allows them to continue working the land without having to worry along with being able to take down any that do get by. I'm getting more worried that we might get overrun before we can get enough fencing up around the animals though. So, to wrap things up. Manpower is our only real issue. That, and we're going to need more fencing equipment and supplies from other places. This area will become dry pretty soon between us and you here in Lake Jackson. That is our status. With that, I bid you adieu. Someone please get me a beer."

Michael looked over at the next speaker and nodded. Gerald Tannert got up reluctantly. Once at the head of the table, he took a minute. "Hello. My name is Gerry. Bear with me please. Public speaking is not my thing." He coughed and then continued. "I guess my job is to be in charge of our aircraft and the fuel situation. Um…the fuel at the fire department is in great shape. I mean, it's almost full so I have no issues for our one helicopter. It wouldn't take all that much to refuel your three too, Bert. I would prefer not too though. Just in case and no offense sir." Bert nodded in understanding. "I have a solution though."

He took another minute to consult his notes. "There is an airfield nearby. Only a few miles up the road. You probably saw it earlier when we went back and forth." Tommy Gun gave his affirmative head shake. "I suggest that we have a Humvee and troop carrier roll up there in the morning along with your gunships. We can check it out first before the Chinook arrives. No use in putting that bird in a possible line of fire without knowing what to expect. That's all I have. I'll get with the bird drivers later over a few dozen beers." Laughter rose up from that as he walked away.

Bert asked Michael if he could talk again. Michael was more than happy to let him. "Just a quick thing. We're leaving in the morning. But! A great many men want to stay behind and help out. You know us military types. Always wanting to see the world and experience new things. Anyway. I'm also leaving behind two of the Seals. Terrell Jackson and Jeremy Turnball are staying to assist you in training. Some of you might not need it but most of you will. They can teach you how to shoot, scout, fight, stage security, and work as teams for infiltration and execution when needed. Every regular civilian needs to be trained as if they were to be soldiers; to some extent. It is the only way to help ensure our survival. It will be a long time before we can walk around freely without having a gun at the ready. We have to accept it. Terry is especially good at hand to hand. By far the best I've ever seen. I like Gerry's idea about the airfield. We'll head that way first thing and then go home. It's good to have so many new friends. I really hope we can acquire a nation of you. Thank you again." Bert gave way to Michael for the end of all the speeches.

"Well people. No more speeches. Why don't we discuss some of our issues over dinner? Maybe someone has a few good ideas. The last thing I've got to say is; let's eat. Once again, the good people of Hoghenheiferz; Tad, Dave, and Dave Jr., have set up one hell of a grub line. Get to eatin'."

Chapter 8

Lake Jackson, TX.

Sunday morning, October 27th

A bevy of activity occurred while Bert and most of his Corpus crew were getting ready to return to the Naval Air Station via the local airfield. They had much to tell the others and new ideas to explore. The hustle and bustle brought a few uninvited visitors, but they were not an issue that couldn't be overcome. Shots would ring out every so often. Very few of them unsuppressed. To keep the noise down as much as possible.

It was only seven in the morning, but people were milling all over the now completely fenced in three blocks. The volunteers had done a great job of finishing the last bit before everyone went to bed. They would continue today and work on the next. It was a nice sized neighborhood so there was plenty of construction to be done. Coffee was dispersed quite liberally while eggs, bacon, and toast were delved out. The same was happening at Wal-Mart. Of course, all of their cooking and eating was done inside at the grill. Membership had its privileges and all that. Everyone enjoyed the bread while it lasted. Soon they would have to start making their own. Along with killing a pig for bacon. That would be a while. They needed to breed more.

Once done, Bert's crews were packing up to go. Only about one third of them were returning to Corpus. Most were staying. There was a lot of work to be done to keep this area secure and scavenging had to continue on a bigger scale and further out to retrieve the needed materials. Since they were to proceed on from the airfield, both Humvees and both troop carriers would go instead of just one and one. On top of this though, four vehicles and a trailer holding a fuel storage tank would tag along. The big truck with the storage tank also had its own tank filling up half the bed of it. This tandem would bring back a little more aviation fuel for the medical helicopter in case of need. Think ahead. That's what geeks do.

"Morning, Bert. Everyone almost ready?" Michael walked up and shook his hand heartily.

"I believe so. How many of your men are going? I noticed your boys gearing up."

"Yeah. They didn't want to pass up the opportunity to get some close-up views of whatever might be there. They always enjoyed the air show out at Ellington Field each year. You know boys and jets. It's an ingrained DNA thing, I guess. I know I got the bug too when I was younger." Michael watched as Aaron and Wayne kissed their mother goodbye. All while loading more guns and ammo into the Dodge dually they had acquired from their neighbor Chugg on that fateful first day. That brave veteran was a tribute to this once great nation. "I think about a dozen men and women have volunteered to go to the airfield. I'm sure we could use whatever we find."

"Never know what you might need, right? Can everyone be ready in ten minutes?" Bert was wanting to get moving.

Michael looked around and saw the last of his people loading up into the pickups. "It looks like they might be ready now." Just as he said that, Gerry walked up to confirm.

"Hey Michael. Everyone is good to go. All I have to do is get over to Wal-Mart and fire up my bird."

"I'll go with you. Get my birds rolling too. Michael. It's been a real pleasure. We simply must do it again soon. Or whenever there's time." He shook Michael's hand and jumped into a truck with Gerry, Davis, and Steve, along with Vinny and his two Seals. On the way by, he gave his men the go ahead to move out.

Once all the birds were in the air, the Cobra and Apache moved quickly towards the airstrip. It wasn't large like a big city but could accommodate larger aircraft when needed. The Dow Chemical corporate jets came and went all the time. Either taking big-wigs or just regular employees back and forth between Louisiana, Michigan, and New York. The Brazoria County Airport could be seen within just a couple minutes of liftoff. Captain Thomas 'Tommy Gun' Blair and Major Pete 'Dragon Rider' Hammond caught up to the caravan just as they got off the freeway and made the U-turn back to Highway 220 that led to the airport.

They hovered as the group made the way back down the feeder and stayed over them the two miles down the next road. Stopping just short of the entrance, they talked it all out really quick. It looked deserted and no one was answering the phone or any radio call. Tommy Gun would take a look down one side of the field while Dragon Rider went around the other. They would crisscross, come back, and see what could be seen. It didn't take long before Dragon called back.

"I see a couple bogies. They think they're hiding. I got a glimpse of a few people inside the control tower. Couldn't tell if they were good or bad guys. No one fired at me at least."

"Yeah, copy that. Several infected meandering across the field. Aimless for now but they'll come running if there's any gunfire. A couple of them looked up as I went by." Tommy was trying to get a better look into the control tower on his way by. *Ping! Ping! Crack!*

"Gawd-dammit! I'm sick of taking potshots from dumbasses. Twice in two days." He veered away from the tower rather quickly. Getting out of the field of fire, he moved back toward the convoy. Along with Dragon.

"Hey, Vinny. They might need you boys here. Wanna play soldier?" Tommy had gotten to be friends with Vinny over the last week and liked to trade jabs with him.

"Well, you know us Seals. Always having to save the world when flyboys like you get in trouble. Or cause it. We're on our way. We'll set down on the back side of the convoy and hop out." The Chinook moved up into position.

"10-4. We'll keep overwatch as usual."

Knowing that the bad guys saw which way the birds flew off, Vinny made an educated calculation. His specialty was tactics and leadership, so no one moved until he decided how and where. After assessing the situation, he decided on a multiple pincer move around behind them and up the other side of the airfield. Or at least as behind them as possible. He staged a special operator with each small group at key locations around the perimeter. Not having a hell of a lot of trained personnel left him with only six teams total. All he had was himself, Jim Lee, and his other Seal Giovanni 'Papa' Papadopolis. Davis and Steve were the only others that had any level of special operations experience in killing. Davis Masters was a former Army Ranger while Steve Hull was a former Marine Force Recon. Only one group would be without someone experienced. The airstrip took up the majority of the small airport so that far side wouldn't have to be covered.

Each of the teams were to stay stationary but cut through the fence and be on the ready. Vinny had two marines with him while one of his Seals, Jim Lee Hooker, was on the complete opposite side of the airfield waiting. They had all synchronized their watches beforehand and set a time to move. There were still a couple minutes left before the other groups would create a diversion. This was the part Vinny always hated. The waiting. Talk about suckville. The adrenaline was palpable.

"All right, boys. Thirty seconds. Let's get this shit done so I can get home for some *Call of Duty* before the servers go down for good." The others laughed some, unheard by Vinny, and prepared for war.

Pop! Pop! Pop! Gunshots sounded from the next group down. Then a grenade went off from the next. Another grenade from the far team and then some more shots from the last of the four. The idea had been to stagger the distractions so whoever was inside believed it was a large group instead of several small ones. Several men came running out towards the sounds with assault rifles in hand. Completely disorganized, they spread out and looked around at nothing. They had no idea what was coming or from where.

Each team moved inside the fence line and got into position behind the closest building. The plan was to stay in place and periodically make noise to draw them further out. While they did this, Jim Lee and Vinny's groups would move toward the tower and try to rescue any hostages. It was a big airport for so few men, on either side, to cover. Two of the teams moved up along the sides of a couple hangars, another covered the two office buildings nearby, while the other snuck into the fuel depot. Those going to the fuel quickly took cover.

Two guards were nervously covering the fuel. They had their weapons at the ready but didn't know where the conflict was coming from next. Two of the men would come up either side while the third in the group would cover them all. Steve was leading this group and would move in as an example. He was a stout man of just under six foot tall but very firmly built. Even in his late forties. Working as a process operator at the plants had helped keep him healthy. They both reached the end of the rows at roughly the same time but only Steve had it easy. As his man was taken down with a choke hold and then a broken neck, the other happened to turn around at the wrong time.

Three steps away, the scruffy looking redneck turned and with surprise tried to raise his rifle. The navy ensign was able to stop the rifle from coming all the way up with his hands but took a right cross to the chin as he did it. The bad guy was so much bigger than the ensign that the hit laid him out cold. The large man was able to pull his knife out and proceeded to move toward cutting his throat. Before he could, the third man in their group fired a short burst into his chest. The man was dying quickly but as he went down, he drove his knife into the Navy Ensign's sternum. Right up to the hilt. The poor man was dead in an instant. The only consolation was that he was unconscious at the time. He never felt a thing.

"Damn. Poor kid. I didn't know him well, but I liked him." Steve had the other man take watch while he called over the radio. "Man down. I repeat. Man down. Southeast side near the fuel depot. Depot secured." They both took up positions and kept watch.

"Copy that. Man down. Watch your six, Steve. I hope this will be over soon." Vinny cursed silently to himself. Keying his mic again, he spoke, "Jim Lee. Let's get this done. Moving up now."

"Roger. Moving." Jim Lee and his crew came up the opposite side of the tower and building. He was going to be coming through the adjoining building and secure the tower from that side. Once they had moved through without incident, they set up another diversion. A small amount of C-4 explosives blew the doors off to the tower itself while they stayed hidden and waiting. Within a minute, two more scruffy looking rednecks peeked around the doorframe. Jim Lee held his crew off for another few seconds. Both of the heads became bodies as they moved into the room followed by a third. Directing his men, Jim Lee and the other two all stood up and each took a different man down. Three shots, three bodies on the ground. From there, they took up stations to cover both exits from the room.

"You're clear, sir. I think they should be plenty distracted. Probably trying to figure out how to get past me. Or go out your way." Jim Lee mused.

"Copy that. I hear already footsteps coming." Vinny waited till someone burst out of the door. *Damn*, Vinny thought. He almost shot a civilian. A man came running out that seemed out of place. He was wearing shorts and a Hawaiian shirt. Dried blood was down the side of his head and he had a pair of broken glasses on. Vinny grabbed the guy and dragged him around the side. Right on his heals a scumbag came bounding through the door. *Pfft!* One suppressed shot through his head. No extra sound.

Calming the man down, Vinny asked him, "You're safe now. We're here to help. How many are we dealing with?"

"Four? Yeah. There's four of them upstairs still. Three went down the other staircase toward the building. When they left in a hurry and the others were distracted, I ran."

"Those three are dead. My boys took care of them already."

"Thank God. They've been holding us there for two days. Those pieces of shit killed Kenny. Just because he couldn't teach them how to fly.

That's what they want. Beat on us till we started to teach them the basics. That's all most of us knew. Just basics, man. Only Tom knows how to fly so they don't know shit yet. Not enough time." The man was talking rather quickly in fear.

"All right. Calm down. You're safe now. We have many men and some choppers. We'll get you out of here, but you have to stay until we get the others out. Okay?"

"Yeah. I can do that."

Vinny looked over to the younger Marine with him. "Watch over him." Turning to the other, he said, "On me. Watch my six."

The second man nodded and got ready. Vinny opened the door and moved aside in case of fire. Nothing. Inside they went and cautiously moved up the staircase. At the top, he peeked his head over and saw where each man was. Just as he moved back, a shot zinged over his head.

"Jim. I need you up the other side. Can you do it?" Vinny touched his comm.

"On it boss." Jim Lee left one of his guys to watch the other door while he and the other moved into the staircase. They got halfway up when a shot pinged off the wall. Ducking back, they waited. Another shot, then a few more. Then Jim heard an audible click. An empty magazine. He quickly moved up the stairs. Spotting a piece of scum trying to reload, he double-tapped the man's upper torso and made it to the top of the stairs. He peeked over the top and almost fell trying to make it back down. Shots were zeroing in on him.

"Three left, boss. They know I'm here."

"Got it, Jim. Good job. I'm going to try to get their attention and hold onto it. Take your suppressor off. When I hear your first shot, I'll pop up and help. Got it?"

"On you, boss. I'll be ready."

Moving so the 'villains' could hear him clearly, he started to work them. "Hey! Scumbags! You might wanna give up. You're all that's left. You three. Everyone else is dead." Vinny had been getting reports from the other teams. Several more tangos were down along with a second one of their own. One of the regular Army men, without much experience, had walked by a port-a-potty being used for some small construction near one of the hangars. Unfortunately, it had been occupied. The shitbird had popped out and put a few bullets in the man's back before he even heard the door swing shut. The next man put him down, but it was already too late.

"Get the fuck out of here or we'll kill these guys. You have no authority here. This airport is

ours now. No law anymore but what we make it."
The man talking was a short, fat man with a
skullet; no hair on top but long in the back. The
other two looked related but taller. Probably just as
dumb, too.

"This is still America, pal. Morality still
rules here. Actual laws or not. You're in the wrong
and I won't allow that to be the new rule of law.
Zombies or not. Lay down your weapons or die
where you stand. Those are the terms." Just for
fun, Vinny shot over their heads.

"Fuck you!" They shot back towards him.
All three of them. That's the only opening Jim Lee
needed. He popped up and shot the two
Neanderthals. They went down like two sacks of
potatoes. Skullet turned his way and started firing.
Yelling about his boys. This gave Vinny a chance.
He moved quickly up and into the room. The little
man started to turn back and met a .45 Caliber
barrel in the snout.

"Hi there. Put it down. Now." The guy
dropped the weapon but still had a smirk on his
face as if he was still in control; his nose pouring
blood from the hit.

"Now what, hero? What the hell are you
gonna do?"

Vinny smirked right back at him. "Us? Nothing."

"Nothing?"

"Nope. I'm going to walk away in a second." Vinny backed up and put his gun away. He had backup, so he wasn't worried about Skullet. "Them, on the other hand. Hmmm. Good luck." He turned to look at the five men that had been huddled on the floor a minute ago. "Gentlemen. When you're done doing whatever you're going to do, please meet me downstairs. We have some things to discuss." They all nodded and started to surround Skullet.

Vinny walked downstairs with the rest of his men. They all met up near the bottom of the tower while a few of them kept watch. The biters had gotten much closer but so far they were munching on the bodies the farthest away. A fitting end to scum. Bert, the helicopters, and all the others moved up into the airfield too. The birds landed near the fuel depot to top off.

"No, no! Please! Don't!" They all looked up just as a figure took a swan dive out the broken window of the control tower. "Nooooooo...!" Splat. Cleanup on aisle three. Skullet didn't need to worry about his hair anymore. Bert walked up just as the men from the tower came through the door.

"Sorry about that, gentlemen. We all decided that was a good end to him. We'll still need to clean up the tower later but...the scavengers can have what's left of that. Anyway. Thank you all. My name is Thomas McClain. Call me Tom. I was managing this field when hell happened. Then these dumbasses came along. What can we do for you now that you have saved us all?"

"I think Vinny would have done worse to him, but I understand. No judgment here. Well sir, my name is Major Bertram Bharata. I am the ad-hoc person in charge of this ragtag group. They put me here, not a self-appointed role. We need fuel to start. I've got to get my birds back down to Corpus Christi. Beyond that, I am hoping that we, as in you and the group that is growing in Lake Jackson can come to some agreement for your future." As they talked, Steve and a few others carried their fallen men back to the trucks. Everyone was solemn as they carried on with that bit of sad business.

"I'm sorry for the men you lost helping us. I wish there was more I could do or say."

"I appreciate it, Tom."

"We'd be happy to meet with the others when able. If you vouch for them, glad to meet 'em."

"That's good news. A couple of their people are here with us now. If you don't mind, we'll just refuel and move out. I've got a lot to do down south."

"It's been a pleasure." He turned to Vinny to shake his hand and thank him also.

"Same here sir. I'll leave you in Steve and Davis's hands. Good luck." With that, he moved out towards the Chinook. The men were stored for burial later; strapped down for the trip. They fueled up the birds and trucks, then headed out to Corpus Christi. It was to be a long trip.

A lone man laid amongst the scrub brush a few hundred yards away. Looking through high-powered binoculars, he was noting info about the small airport. Wearing forest green camouflage, one would be hard-pressed to make him out unless you were close enough to smell his chewing gum. Dressed in casual but dark clothing, he gave no indication of who he worked for.

Once the larger group started to move off from the airfield, he prepared to leave. Before he made his call to his handlers, the watcher ensured the helicopters were well away from being able to spot him. When he felt safe enough, he inched back down the small hill and out of sight.

Shouldering his weapon that had constantly been at the ready, he pulled out a Satellite phone. The one thing that might stay working during the apocalypse. As long as the big boys kept the machinery in orbit and the power on. No longer worried about people tracking them, what with the apocalypse and all, he keyed in a number.

"Control" was the only answer to the call.

"Gopher One here."

"Go Gopher One."

"Large group with helos on the move. Unable to track them but heading in a Southwest direction. Second smaller group stationed here at the local airfield and staying. One bird and some trucks left with fuel heading straight South. I assume it is the Lake Jackson locals we've been hearing about. Airport is firmly under local control. They took out my opposition. Advise."

"Stand by, Gopher One." While he waited, he spat out his gum and grabbed a new piece. A full minute went by before they came back on the line. Amazingly, he had to still listen to Muzak while on hold, even during Zombiegeddon. What the hell was wrong with people? Did they actually think someone *wanted* to listen to this shit?

"Do not engage. You are to stay within sight distance of the Lake Jackson group and keep us informed. Troop size, civilian numbers, vehicles, any aircraft they have, and what kind of condition the group is in. Anything useful for the future."

"Copy that. Anything else?"

"That is all"

"Roger that. Out."

After putting the phone away, he gathered what little gear he had. Rustling in the tree line dragged his attention toward the sound. An old woman zombie started toward him and stopped. He assessed her as she assessed him. Animal instinct told her that the man was dangerous. Not worth the meal. She turned around and shuffled back into the trees. Smiling, the man moved off back toward the highway but well off the road. He knew the general area they headed and walked back to his motorcycle. The company had provided a stealth type bike. Very low noise so he wouldn't be heard. Jumping on, he took off. He had a job to do. Not really much different from what he used to do for the CIA. Blend when needed; watch and report as necessary. Stay on mission.

Chapter 9

Near Brownsville, TX.

Commander Nolan Brink was in command of the Coast Guard Cutter as they rounded the end of their run. He and the colonel had made it back without incident the night before with two men from Lake Jackson. Packed with some board games for the children and riding in style, they had commandeered a decked-out Lincoln Navigator. Upon arrival, Brink checked in with Captain Tonia Parnell and then headed towards his men at the Coast Guard station. Being late that night, he got a quick rundown of what had happened from Grace and then headed for his bunk. It might be a long day tomorrow.

Turns out it was. They were approaching Brownsville when he spotted a yacht on fire near the Mexico border. Coming up slowly, he made sure his crew was ready for whatever. Thinking ahead, or behind, in this case, he made a radio call to one of their choppers. The Coast Guard had been ambushed last week so he was taking no chances. Once the helicopter got overhead, he had them do a flyby at altitude.

Seeing nothing to hold them back, Brink moved toward the boat. He could see several people in the water and a few more still on the boat scared shitless. His crew got the lifeboat down and proceeded to perform rescue duties. As the cutter moved closer Brink could see the survivors on the boat were no longer in need of help. They were turned and had been wanting the fresh meat in the water. So, like cats, the infected didn't like water much either. He could also see a few floating bodies nearby but was unable to tell whether they had been healthy people before drowning. With the way the infected on the boat were acting, they had been munchers that had braved the water but paid the price.

It took a while to pick up all the survivors in the water while Brink watched the boat burn. Zombies and all. No need in wasting bullets on them. Once everyone was on board, he heard their story. A few had gone ashore for supplies. One had come back infected but not told anyone until it was too late. They had infected a few of their family during the night and downhill it went from there. Gunfire had erupted, and something sparked a fire. Hence, overboard they went. Well, more survivors for their already gigantic group.

They continued on to the border to finish their patrol. Several people could be seen on the docks, fishing like normal. The only difference was, at each beachhead, security had been set up in case of feverhead assault. It was good to see people trying to get on with life. Unsure of their allegiance and not wanting to put his own people in harm's way, they started back up the coast. The helicopter was still tracking them when it radioed down to Commander Brink.

"You've got company coming. Two fast boats on your six. Definitely armed. Look like cartel."

"Got it. I'll call in the nearest boat for help. Can you provide cover?"

"We've got our .50 Cal and that's it. But we got you. Just say the word."

"If they fire, unleash hell on their ass." Switching channels, he called, "Come in Chief Grace."

"Go for Grace."

"Vector on me ASAP. Got two cartel fast boats on my ass. I've got civilians on board."

"On my way, sir."

One of the boats moved out to the right of the cutter and held steady while the second continued to pace close behind. No moves had been made yet, but the tension was building. Command Chief Grace was still a good fifteen minutes out from rendezvous. Brink was hauling ass his direction just in case. Watching the shores was a distant memory in light of the situation. Things suddenly got dicey when another helicopter came on the scene. This one from land just to the left and ahead of them. Now they were outnumbered; two boats and a chopper to one cutter and a rescue helicopter. Not good odds. Still no moves were made.

"Calling all boats and air support in the area. Commander Brink here. This is a mayday situation."

"This is Captain Lighter. What's your situation sir?"

"Got two cartel fast boats and now a gunship pacing us. Requesting assistance immediately."

"I've got two more birds in the air near us. We can all be there within ten minutes. Hold steady sir. Good luck."

"Roger. C'ya soon."

Chief Grace met up with them back up near South Padre Island and pulled around next to Commander Brink. At the same time, the other two rescue choppers showed up. As with the other one, they also only had a single .50 Caliber at the door. Still no moves toward hostility on either side. Preparations were made for war along the way. Belts were set up near the mini-guns, extra magazines given out, grenades pinned on each Coastie, and even a rocket launcher on each boat was readied. No chances were given. The pressure was running high in anticipation, but the crews were ready and steady. The helicopters may not have had much in the way of firepower, but the Cutters were set for a small war.

A couple more tense minutes later, Captain Lighter showed up. Now the cartel was vastly outnumbered themselves, but they just circled the group with the boats and helicopter. In their minds, it was a show of force, but the concept was lost on the Coast Guard when they were now the big bad in the neighborhood. After a few more ticks, the cartel boys in the boats flipped them all the bird and then took off south again, along with their whirly bird. Immediately the radio became full of questions back and forth.

"What the hell was all that? I would have bet a million bucks we would be in a firefight a long time ago." Brink was flabbergasted.

"We should chase them down and arrest them, sir." Chief Grace still thought this was the old world and law was king.

"Calm down Grace. We have civilians aboard and I guarantee we would be running right into an ambush."

"It's our job to bring them in. We can't let them get away."

"Stand down, Chief Grace. It is no longer our job to police the seas. We've been through this already. You have to change your mindset to the new reality. We don't arrest anymore. It is a case of live and let live or kill now. This doesn't warrant either. I am still in charge. Unless you and your crew want to take off on your own. Your choice."

"No, sir. You're in command."

"Then for now, they are gone. Let's get back to Corpus. Something else is happening, I fear. We need to regroup. This could be bad in the future."

"Yes sir. I understand."

"We got your six, sir." Captain Lighter maneuvered his boat to the end of the others and brought up the rear. The helicopters all patrolled the skies on the way back.

Chapter 10

Corpus Christi

During the Coast Guards ocean fun time, the daily excursions from the Naval Air Station were still going out. Usually three or more groups moving out further and further gathering supplies. The Corpus Christi group had grown quite large over the first week. One particular party built of two Humvees and a Deuce and a Half full of volunteers were currently at the docks pouring through the area shipping containers. This was going to be many days' worth of work. This place was huge.

Today was their first time here and the task was daunting. Two-man crews were opening each container, so each had a backup. They had run into no resistance upon arrival. Only one person was on the scene and no zombies to be found. Without a visible food source, they had no reason to try and get inside the fencing. A lone security guard knew what had been happening and found no reason to leave. Plenty of food and water was in the offices and surrounding units that made up the docks. He was most helpful to them after they established who they were.

Ben Casey was another former Army dogface that had served in Grenada, retired out after his twenty, and was happy to help those trying to rebuild. He had pledged his loyalty to their cause easily but would stay where he was. The docks needed someone, and he was still the best man for the job. He decided this would be his permanent duty station. The few large ships docked nearby held only a few of the original crews. Each of them waved, some came down to meet the new people, and others cried in gratitude that there were others out there. Most wanted to go with them when they left while a few stayed behind to help with the security of the docks. They knew there was still much here to protect and was currently safe from the infected. There were a few vehicles around they could 'borrow' when they left, and more items could be loaded at that time.

Ben moved with them trying to sift through the manifests as they went. Some of it was difficult to read, handwriting not always being taught or learned correctly. They had opened containers with clothing, computers, televisions, food, water, sodas, chips, etc. It was about the fifteenth container they came to that was almost passed up. The manifest said it was lawnmower parts. Not exactly something they needed. Ben thought they might look anyway. He had a thought that he wasn't sharing. They walked in and started cracking open the many boxes. Yep. Lawnmower parts. At least on top of each.

"Holy shit! Looky here." One of the ensigns exclaimed.

"I knew something didn't smell right. A hunch paid off. Enjoy boys. You see this a lot with any type of machine parts shipment. That is if the right looker is looking. It is usually a cartel or arms broker thing." Ben laughed and walked toward the next container pair.

A couple more pairs of the Navy and Marines came over to find out what the big deal was. They had stumbled upon a whole container of shoulder mounted rocket launchers. Where they came from might never been found out now. Those that used to keep track of that stuff were now long gone. Or nowhere to help at least. This was grade 'A', made in America, military hardware. Obviously stolen and somehow on a shipping container headed toward Bogota, Columbia. Someone had sold some serious firepower to a cartel. Awesome. Frakkin' traitors.

Well, to hell with the cartels. However many were still alive, they sure as hell couldn't get the weapons now. This turned into a great day for the good guys. Never want to have to use these destructive tools but needs must. All the lawnmower parts were gathered together and left in the container while the storage boxes of launchers were loaded up onto the big truck to take back to the Air Station.

Farther away, down another line of containers, four other 'shoppers' were trying to open up some of those that were stacked two and three high. The idea was to look into each ahead of time and determine which they would bring down to exploit later. Two people would jump into a scissor lift and pop open the doors. If it looked worth it, they would climb out of the basket and do a quick search through. If not, they moved on to the next. Quick and easy; so they thought. They had gotten three checked out so far with two being very lucrative and to be brought down immediately. Kubota generators of various sizes were stacked to the top of each and ready for some tender loving care. Brand new and straight from Japan. A little oil and diesel fuel to make a lot of people happy when the lights do finally go out. And diesel should be plentiful for a while. Of good use, at least till they can get solar power going. Ideas have been flying since the beginning of the end. Geeks do a lot of thinking.

As they moved the lift over to the fourth box, the controller's hand slipped, and they banged into the front of it. They both half bent over the railing from the sudden stop and yelled expletives. The controller mumbled out a '*Sorry*' and backed them up a little to be able to open the doors. While cutting off the lock, shuffling could be heard on the other side.

Hollering down to the others of possible infected, they opened the doors while backing the lift up. Whatever was in there had been holed up for at least a week, so they didn't expect any quick movement. They went really slow with the opening until it was wide enough and then moved back quickly. No sense on getting bitten while in the air and unable to get away. The stench told them that a few were dead at the least. Quite overpowering. Once the doors were wide open, and nothing jumped out, they flashed their lights around inside. Bodies were scattered all over with no movement. It looked like a coyote had been using the container to smuggle illegals over the border. What did they care how many died when they already had their money? So many dead. Then something peeked out from behind a cardboard box. A young man, with dirt and grime all over, maybe of the teen variety, started to move out.

"Come on out son. We're here to help." One of the guys started to unbuckle his harness to help the young man out. Inch by inch the boy moved towards the doors. Obviously scared, the teenager was still hunched over as he walked. Then he started running. Rather quickly for someone stuck in a box for however long. At first, the guys were surprised, then…

"Move back! Now!" The helper was trying to get as far back into the lift as possible. Before they could get out of reach, the boy had leapt into the basket and was barreling over the man not tied in. They both went over the rail and fell the two stories down to the ground. A shriek rang out of the zombie boy, but he recovered rather fast and tried to crawl over to the ensign.

"Fuck me! My legs are broken! Help!" The poor man was trying to crawl away, seeing the zombie still trying to eat. Luckily, the other two broke off from their container at the bottom and ran over. They each put several bullets into the kid just as he reached an ankle to grab.

"Oh, thank God. I have too much to live for. Okay. Maybe not but I still want to live." After grunting and turning over onto his back, he said, "Get me the hell out of here. I'm useless now."

The others called over for transport. Being smart in how Captain Parnell put the crews together, a medic came over and tried his best to reset the ensign's legs. Having done all he could, he stinted them and called over some lift help. They put him into the back of the truck and sent it on its way back to the Naval Air Station. They had a couple doctors that hadn't seen any action lately but a skinned knee on a child. The only good thing about this for the ensign was now he could play games with the kids all day for a while. Around rehab that is. Once the truck was gone, they all went back to work. The difference would be that now every container would be brought down before they opened it. This would take much longer but give them the ability to work safer. Not like they didn't have all the time in the world. What was left of the world, anyway?

The rest of the day they tried to get through as many metal containers as possible. They found one more that was hiding a boatload of ammunition of many varying calibers. They loaded all of this onto the truck as well. Food and water were loaded in the space left and shoved into parts of the Humvees. It was a very good day for scavenging. Wait till Bert and Vinny hear about this.

Chapter 11

Early Afternoon, Lake Jackson

Aaron and Wayne were still running around looking for parts but had decided to go farther than any previous excursion. The thought had occurred to Wayne that the local hardware and lumber store in Brazoria had probably been forgotten. He was supposed to start working there during the winter break but that was never going to happen now. The other guys were all heading in opposite directions, hoping to gather as much as they could in short amounts of time.

Each of the original group took a few more volunteers with them today to help. Aaron and Wayne had a second follow pickup and both of them were dragging trailers behind them. They rolled down Highway 332 and past William's house. This brought up tears to Aaron and Wayne's eyes since they had lost their grandmother that first week there. A tragic death at the hands of a psychopathic redneck. William had taken care of him, but it had been too late. Grandma Kay was buried in the back. Holding back his tears, Aaron made a mental note to call William and make sure there wasn't anything he needed on the trip back.

It only took a few more minutes to drive into Brazoria. The damage could be seen everywhere. Looting had been rampant during the last week. The bank had a small fire inside still. Probably from someone trying to blow the safe and not having a clue how to use the explosives correctly. The grocery store was shot up and windows broken also. Hard to fault someone for wanting to grab whatever food they could but the bank thing was just plain stupid. What the hell good was money? At least rob someone for the gold and silver. They might be useful later but paper money? Idiotic. There were several spots in the area that they could guess those geniuses might live. Hell, it was probably their dumbass cousins. Wastes of flesh that won't get jobs and just mooch off others. These thoughts were spoken aloud between them as they pushed on out the other side of Brazoria to the store.

Rolling up to the McCoy's storefront hadn't taken them much time. Very few vehicles were in the way since most people had either crashed or tried to get as far away from the hell as possible that first day. They parked a little away from the front doors and got out to assess the situation. The glass doors looked to be mostly intact still. Wide open but glass still in them. The two men that came with them, Ron and Bill, would go in first with Aaron and Wayne watching their backs. The older men felt a sense of responsibility to watch over the young boys. Even though Michael's boys had already seen more action than they had. Aaron had seen action at Academy and they had both been in a battle at Chugg's that first day. Reality had slammed an anvil down upon their world in a very fast heartbeat.

Setting up at the doors, Ron and Bill moved through the store. Aisle by aisle, most of the store was pretty easy to go through. You could walk right down the middle of the store and look both ways. Halfway down, McCoys had changed up their style and they had to break up for the rest. Finishing up, they both started back up to the front and called out to the boys.

"All clear in here. All that's left is the lumber area and outside." Bill had said while dropping his weapon back onto the strap.

"Let's clear that then. We need to get a move on." Aaron headed toward the back left where the lumber counter was.

"Hey. I'm going to hit the head." Ron went back towards the rear of the store. He was almost there when Wayne yelled at him.

"Be sure to check the restroom before you whip it out."

"Ha, ha, ha." Ron had just opened the men's room door when an infected burst out of the women's room and jumped onto his back. This drove him down and inside the door. Out of sight from everyone else that started running and yelling.

"Ahhhh! Get off me! Ow!" Ron was scrambling to turn around, but it was already too late. The twenty-something girl had taken a chunk out of his neck and wouldn't stop. Bill was the first to reach him and beat the girl off of Ron. Aaron made it there in time to put a bullet through her brainpan. Bill tried to stifle the blood loss, but she must have taken out a major artery. Ron was stuttering "Mommy" and died within just a couple minutes.

After a few moments to collect themselves, Wayne cleared the restroom just in case. Aaron did the same for the women's. Bill was still mourning and hadn't moved. The boys found some canvas and tried to get Bill to help them wrap Ron up. Bill was gone. He couldn't even seem to talk. Maybe didn't even have the ability to hear them. They left him there and started toward the lumber counter again. There was still store to clear. Slowly they moved to the door frame and proceeded on sided by side through the opening. Once through, they turned to cover their side. Aaron looked over the counter and found nothing on the other side. Having the short side of the small area, he met Wayne at the other end. This held the door going outside.

Being normal storefront doors, they had glass in the upper part, so it was easy to see through. They still cautiously moved out and stalked the large outside aisles of wood. Not wanting to be caught unawares again, they actually walked along each of the long rows and checked into every open spot. The boys planned to live as long as possible and had learned all of their lessons the hard way lately. Once done, they found the front gate unlocked and open. Just in case, they moved together to their Dodge Dually. Wayne checked the other truck Bill had had the good sense to take the keys out, so he couldn't move it yet. Jumping in with Aaron, they drove the truck through the lumber yard and parked it near the doors but close to the first row of wood.

They jumped out, took the keys, and walked inside to start loading up everything they possibly could. Aaron walked by the restroom to check on Bill and saw he was still there in mourning. Leaving Bill to it, he and Wayne moved through each aisle and grabbed boxes of stuff. Everything from screws and washers on down to cables and wire strippers. After a while, they both needed a break. They found the water and soda and walked outside to the truck. Turning on the radio, they killed about fifteen minutes or more before deciding it was time to get back to work. For two boys only sixteen and seventeen, their sense of work ethic was large.

Walking back inside, they both went for a piss before starting back up. Getting back there, they noticed that Bill was gone. So was Ron's body though. Performing their business first, they moved on through the store and towards the front looking and calling for Bill. Once out the front doors, they still found no sight of either of them. Not that Ron could move but still.

"Good God. You don't think the dead are coming back, do you? Maybe Ron came back and bit Bill?" Wayne actually looked worried. None of this was supposed to happen in the first place. How would they know if this wasn't the next evolution in the virus? That would suck. Hard.

"We don't need a *Romero* situation."

"Huh?"

"Romero. As in Dawn of the Dead."

"Oh. I got you. No way I'm hiding in a mall. That doesn't go well in any movie I've ever seen."

"That's true."

"Hell no. We have enough problems without the dead trying to eat us too."

"No way that's happening. Right?" Aaron got scared too.

Neither of them wanted to call out in case there were any infected in the area. No need to bring on any party crashers. Still not finding any sign of Bill or Ron, Aaron pulled out his cell.

"Mom. We got a problem."

"Are you okay? Is Wayne hurt?" Mom radar was suddenly in full tilt.

"We're fine mom. We lost Ron though. A small girl took him out when he headed for the bathroom. Really sucked. But now we can't find Bill either. Ron's body and Bill are both gone. And Bill has the keys to the second truck."

"Well crap. What can I do?"

"We're trying to load everything we can onto our truck but the other one is too far to try and load by hand." A thought occurred to him and he turned to Wayne. "Hey Wayne. See if you can figure out that forklift. Maybe we can load some wood onto the F-150. At least we can make it useful."

"Good idea. I'm on it."

"Hey Aaron. I'll see if I can find a volunteer to come and hotwire the truck. Maybe get you some more help. I want you back before dark. I will not lose my boys. I just can't."

"Thanks mom. That would be great. We'll get as much done as we can. Like Steve and Davis say, we'll keep our head on a swivel."

"Be careful and take care of your brother. I love you."

"I love you too mom. See you soon." As soon as he was off the phone, the forklift started moving in jerky motions. It would take a few minutes to get the controls down but Wayne was giving it his all. From there, they did everything they could to get as much plywood loaded onto the truck as possible. All the while watching out for zombies and Bill. They were both still a little scared that maybe the dead were walking after all. Just because they hadn't seen it yet, didn't mean it wasn't happening.

It was 4pm by the time their help arrived. Three more trucks with a couple more trailers. Someone they hadn't met before walked over to the F-150 and had it going within just two minutes. Once he knew it was running, he killed the engine again. No use in wasting gasoline. He came back out from under the dashboard and approached the boys.

"Howdy do my friends. My name is Andres DeMatteo."

"Hi, sir. Good to meet you. Thank you for coming to help out. How did you do that?" Aaron shook his hand with a smile.

"My ill spent youth. I was not a very good boy when I was young. As the tattoos all over my neck can testify. You have nothing to fear from me now though. I served my time many years ago and used to be a model member of society after. At least until society went to hell."

"Didn't fear you at all, sir. If my mom thought enough of you to send you to help, then I wasn't worried. My father taught us to treat everyone fairly until they proved not worthy. You're a welcome godsend as far as I'm concerned. This is my brother, Wayne."

"Howdy back at you sir." Wayne shook his hand like a gentleman also.

"It's good to meet you two. Very unusual for two young men to be so cordial. Impressive. What do you need me to do? We have to get moving, right? Only a couple hours left of daylight."

"We tried to get as much loaded as possible, but we needed help. Our truck is full. I guess we just need to get everyone to grab everything. If it looks useful for power, wiring things, building walls, or even if it might be used as a weapon somehow, let's get it loaded."

"All right. Let's work." Andres jumped into a truck and moved it into the yard. The other truck followed while the third without a trailer set up at the front doors. Throughout the next two hours, a few more infected came near them looking for food and died for not turning around. It was a pretty uneventful time other than that. They left just as the sun was starting to set. Never having seen Bill again.

The small caravan of pickups made it back to the growing Lake Jackson post-apocalyptic neighborhood after sundown. The security details opened up the gates, picking off an intruder or two trying to get in, and re-secured them after. The unloading would proceed the following day though. The wall being erected to enlarge the secure area for living would also continue tomorrow. The last of the workers were inside and preparing for dinner. No work was done shortly after dusk because of the likelihood of attack. No use in putting others in harm's way.

"C'mere you two." Ann ran up to her boys as soon as their truck stopped. Hugging them heartedly, she elicited a few groans of equal love from Aaron and Wayne.

"Ow, mom. I can't breathe." Wayne tried to get out of the hug.

"We're okay. No bites." Aaron patted his mom on the back in assurance.

"You two are getting too old, too quickly. No one your age should have to go through what you've seen and done. It's unnatural." Tears were forming in her eyes.

"It's all good mom. As long as we're together, we got this. We watch each other's backs."

"Good to have you with us again. I'm missing you two a lot lately." Michael had walked up at this time and gave a quick hug to each. "Well, get washed up. Just about time for dinner." He held Ann, knowing her feelings just by looking at her face.

"Got it dad." They both took off to the house their family had chosen.

"I'm so scared for them, Michael. They shouldn't be out by themselves."

"They weren't. It was—unfortunate—what happened but they didn't start out alone. It sounds like they handled things extremely well though. I'm so proud of how they have been taking everything in stride. I know they didn't get that from me."

"Flattery will get you everywhere and you know it." Ann slapped his arm. "Keep them safe. Or I'll kick your ass."

"Yes ma'am." He kissed her deeply and they went towards the big common eating area that had been set up for everyone. They all ate together nowadays. Even those at Wal-Mart eat together each night. Always a different group holding security each night in rotation. That way there was never the same people on guard duty two nights in a row. Michael had established this as their impromptu leader. He had felt it was best for them all to grow as a community. Learning how to be a family was the best thing he had gotten from Ann's side. Something he had never had in his growing up. It was also the best way to keep everyone informed each day. Better than yelling across a large crowd. And their community was getting rather large.

Chapter 12

Almost Back in Corpus Christi

"Sir. I'm getting a distress call from down south. The Army Reserves in Harlingen seem to be having problems." Bert's pilot, Lt. Elvis 'Muttonchop' Bennett called to him through the headset.

"Patch me through." Bert waited a second.

"You're good to go sir."

"This is Major Bertram Bharata of the Navy. What's going on down there?"

"We've got cartel problems, sir. They started trying to bully the citizens down here a few days ago. We intervened a couple times, but they brought more firepower. Right now, we're holed up and just trying to survive. We've got the guns and ammo but not enough people. Only women and children. The cartel killed off what men they had. I'm afraid we don't have long."

"We can be there in twenty. Hold on."

"We'll try." An explosion could be heard over the radio. The man said to someone nearby, "What the hell was that?"

"Just stay alive." Bert said to let the man go.

"Please hurry. Out." The Army signed off.

"Mutt. Contact Dragon and Tommy. Then Captain Parnell. Get them there now."

"On it." With that, all three helicopters took off as fast as possible. Bert contacted Captain Tonia Parnell to direct a couple Humvees of troops to take off from the Naval Air Station in Corpus. They would need boots on the ground with the air power. They could be there within two hours. Air support is almost all Bert could do for now.

The explosion had been the front gate being blown in. Taking with it the two guards on the inside. So much for keeping the warzones overseas. It was here at home now. Just because people can never have enough and always want what others already own. The civilians were herded back into the furthest bunker and locked in tight. Safe unless their protectors all died. Those same protectors were in positions all over the medium sized compound. They were relatively safe and ammo'd up for a long evening.

Several men were scattered around the entrance trying to take potshots into the compound. Even with the gates down, they couldn't progress any more. Their only shot was to try and come in the fence line wherever they could. Men in groups of three moved into two different spots along both sides they could get to. One in each group would cut the wire while the other two watched out in both directions. Almost a great plan.

Just as each group started cutting, lights blazed to life. Blinding them all temporarily, gunfire rang out. The Army had thought of the same ideas as the cartel and were lighting them up. Both literally and figuratively. It might seem an unsound idea in daylight, but these were of the military grade, blindingly bright, variety. It was also the added element of surprise. Rounds ripped into each drug runner; spinning them all around into red mists of afterlife. Only one was still moaning in pain once the gunfire stopped. One well-placed bullet put him down for good.

The lights went out immediately. No use in advertising their placement for too long and inviting cartel members to shoot them. All the noise is bound to bring some Zs their way, too. Hopefully, they'll just munch on the cartel. Fixing the gates would be the next priority.

Silence came over the area. The new guards near the gates could see the vermin moving around out there but they had stopped firing. The men inside used this opportunity to bring forward some bigger guns and restock on their ammunition supplies. Take advantage of the opportunities when they came.

"What the hell are they doing?" Men began talking to each other around the compound. They only had a few dozen Army personnel, but they would do whatever they needed to help civilians in any way possible. These men still knew their duty to what was once a great nation.

"Can't tell."

"Maybe losing those guys around the fence made them think twice."

"I'm thinking more along the lines that they are bringing in heavier weapons. I think we pissed them off. Everyone get in place. This isn't over. These shitheads think they can own whatever they want to. We're still American military, boys." Turning his head to the one woman in his squad, Lt. Packer spoke straight to her. "And lady." Back to them all, "We will kill them all if that is what it takes. We've got help on the way. Just hold the line people. Now get to work."

It stayed silent for several more minutes. Plenty of movement on the outside but no shots of any kind rang towards the men. The complete lack of fire was starting to get to some of those inside. To most of them, this was the first combat they had been involved in. It was unnerving without knowing why.

A growing, grumbling, sound stopped them all in their tracks. As it got louder, the realization of a much bigger problem swept through the squad. Something very large and very heavy was heading their way. The lieutenant sent someone up high with binoculars to get a better look. A few minutes later, the man called back down on the radio.

"Sir. We are in for a world of hurt."

"What do we got?"

"They've got a tank. Don't know what kind yet."

Silently, the Lt. said, "Shit". "How far?"

"A mile or more. It's slow going because of the vehicles on the road. He's rolling over those he can't get around, but it'll be here within fifteen minutes."

"Roger. Just keep an eye on it for me. Out."

"People! Here's the situation." Without gathering everyone for a turkey shoot, he filled them in.

A few minutes later the sound was getting quite loud and then sort of stopped. The engine noise was still there but the tank was no longer rolling. Lt. Packer figured that they were probably going over their battle plan before beginning the assault. Cartel goal number one; wipe them out.

"Lieutenant! Sir!"

"Go for LT."

"It's a damn SEP, sir. They've got a M1A2 SEP. We don't have anything that could damage that, sir."

"Double damn. All right. Stay on station. I need to know everything you see as you see it. Copy that soldier?"

"Sir, yes, sir."

Once again addressing everyone else, Packer said, "Big problem, people. They've got one of the newer tanks. We are screwed if it gets close enough to us. Even our rocket launchers and RPGs couldn't break through it. Anybody have any ideas? I'm all out." Only one voice spoke up.

"Sir. We have one thing. We can use an IED. If I'm correct, it won't have the Urban

Survival Kit attached. Damn government is too cheap to add them to local-use hardware."

"Proudstar. What the hell are you talking about? I'm not up on my tank knowledge."

Jacob 'Proudstar' Bloodfeather was in his wheelhouse now. "Sir. The military deployed these tanks all over the country when the infected started getting to be too much. They always kept a certain amount domestically for civilian actions. With all the budget cuts under the previous president, the Army didn't install the extra armor to protect against explosives on the ground. No real reason to in their minds. Not domestically. This one should be no different. We can take it out with a really good explosive underneath. Finding the right supplies is the only real hard part. And surviving the first round or two from that rather large cannon."

"Give yourself a blue ribbon. Grab whoever and whatever you need. So far, that's our only hope. Go."

The men scrambled to get things done without getting shot. Rather quickly at that. They took about ten whole minutes gathering and came back together near the front again. Proudstar had a disappointed look on his face though.

"Sir. We can't complete the bomb quick enough. I don't think. We can assemble it but the only thing we could use for explosives would be the gunpowder. Or maybe dissembling an RPGs. I just don't believe we have the time, sir."

"All right. Well, what choice do we have? Do it. Commandeer whatever you have to. Just work as quickly as you can." Two minutes later, the engine noise revved up again. "Shit. We just ran out of time. Move back into position. Proudstar! Keep working but be prepared."

"Sir, yes, sir."

"Lieutenant. It's moving again. We have maybe five minutes before it moves into position to at least fire this direction."

"Got it. Hunker down, son. It's gonna be a long one or a very short one. Either way, we fight."

"Yes sir."

The tank rounded the last corner and fired a round into the Army compound. It glanced off a cement building and exploded off target. Luckily it didn't kill anyone, but it blew out a couple eardrums. Seeing how badly it aimed, the M1 squared up to hit the front building. The personnel all moved further away to prepare for what was coming. Just before the next round came, the top part of the beast exploded and flipped off the body. Cartel members just stared in amazement. Large rounds started ripping into the ground all around the tank. Cartel pukes started scrambling for cover.

Suddenly a very loud speaker started blaring *'Fade to Black'* by the Rolling Stones. An equally loud *"Yahoo!"* went through that same speaker. Tommy Gun came rolling sideways around the largest of the cartel goons, firing .50 caliber rounds into scumbag bodies of worthless shitheads. Clearly a master of his aircraft, he was pouring round after round into the bad guys. Going after the smaller groups running from the firefight, Dragon Rider was doing the same mop-up job as him. The cavalry had arrived. Just in time, too. A few more rounds from that big bore cannon would have destroyed everything and killed even the civilians. It only took a few minutes to mow them all down. Once done, the two birds hovered as Bert and his Chinook came in for a landing at the back of the compound. Then Tommy and Dragon landed.

A few of the mid-level cartel bosses had gotten about a mile away. Fleeing like illegal immigrants that just robbed a bank, they took off as soon as the tank blew. Fortunately, they didn't get very far. Knowing that some might get away,

Bert had landed his Seals a few miles away on the way back south.

Vinny and the boys lit up the SUV with their weapons. The rounds made contact but didn't punch through. These boys had the forethought to drive an armored vehicle. Well, they had something for that little problem. Jim Lee pulled out a rocket launcher, aimed, and fired. The SUV did a forward exploding flip and landed on its top. They moved into position around the vehicle, taking care along the way for anyone still alive. The truck was on fire and they could hear someone screaming for help inside. Vinny bent down slowly and cautiously to look inside. He could see a large man trying to get free from being crushed by his driver.

"Please. Help me. I can't move my legs."

"Aww. Sucks to be you."

"I'm begging you. Please get me out of here."

"Yeeeah. I'm thinking not. You're a bad guy. I kill bad guys. Why would I get you out?"

"I can pay you. Gold, platinum, whatever you want."

"Wow. Really? Well that makes all the difference in the world, then. Not! Bye." Vinny got up and walked away.

"Punta! I'll kill you! Your family is dead!"

Vinny pulled out a grenade and was about to toss it into the truck. Thinking about it, he decided not to waste it. Never know when you might need a grenade in the apocalypse. He walked back over there and bent down again.

"Hey. I was fixing to frag you, but I had a change of heart."

"Oh, thank you. Get me out of here."

"Sorry. That's not why I came back. I just figured that putting a bullet in your head was a cheaper option."

"Motherfu…" *Blam!* Brain matter spewed out the back of his head while a giant red hole appeared between his eyes. Vinny looked in for another second or two. Making sure the others were dead, he walked away again. He and his crew moved through the streets towards the Army Reserve Depot. Along the way, they picked up a bunch more civilians that came up to them. Many wanted to hug them and thank them. The women gave them kisses and the few older men left just wanted to shake their hands. They had helped liberate them from evil. It ended up being a good day.

Along the way, several infected tried to come by for lunch but between the Seals and some of the locals, they made short work of them. Once they arrived at the Army Reserve compound, they could see that a temporary barricade had already been set up where the front gates stood. A few zombie bodies lay about but that was to be expected with the fire still brewing on the tank top. Bert was busy talking with Lt. Packer when Vinny walked up.

"All secure, sir."

"Good job, Vinny. Any problems?"

"No sir. Had to use a launcher though. Armored vehicle. Picked up more civilians along the way too. A lot of people are happy with what you've done to secure their future, Lieutenant."

"Well I'm just glad you showed up when you did. Otherwise they would still be in peril. We had nothing to stop that hell on tracks. Except for maybe an IED; but my boy, Proudstar, didn't think we could get that ready in time. I would suggest that y'all keep some of those around in case you run into these tanks. I mean. Since the Army left so many of them laying around the United States and all." Packer said this last with a smile.

"I'm glad we could help. I've got a couple Hummers coming with some backup. Captain Parnell is sending them from Corpus. There is an overabundance of personnel there that can help. We need to arm the citizenry and show them how to protect themselves. This isn't the last time you'll see the cartels. They've always wanted to take over Texas. For some reason they think they deserve to control everyone. I take a great joy in killing each and every one of them. Well, not me personally. Vinny won't let me. Right?"

"Yes, sir. You are the man in charge. The man with the plans. You're too important to be put in the middle."

cough "Yeah, right. I'm just a cog that people are somehow looking to. I'm hoping we can convince the Senator to take over eventually. He's better qualified."

"Excuse me. A senator? Who?" Packer was intrigued.

"Senator Fred Cruz. We just ran into a man that has a big piece of real estate in Southwest Houston with a lot of warehouses. The senator is his guest. All on the up and up. We visited them. Really will be a good friend as days go on."

"Well hot damn. That is good news. He should have been the next president. So, what's next, sir?"

"My boys will stay here and help out for a few days. Once they finally get here that is. Use them as long as you need. Send back the ones that want to come back. We don't stand on ceremony anymore. Those that want to stay in the ranks can, but no one is forced to anymore. And even some of those that still want to stand on tradition want to stick around here and there to help out. Plenty of need out there these days."

"All right. We appreciate the help. I'm hoping we can get some more help from down the way. McAllen has another station and a National Guard unit. I haven't been able to get ahold of anyone yet. Once we're stabilized here, I plan on sending a few units that way. We need to find out what happened." The Lt. had a worried look on his face while speaking about his fellow soldiers.

Bert thought about it for a minute and then said, "Vinny. Do you have any issues with us sticking around for tonight? I was thinking that we can do a flyby in the morning of the stations. Be quicker. What do you think?"

"I go where and when you want boss. This is what I do. Protect your ass—ets. I think it's a good idea."

"All right then. Can you let our flyboys know so they can batten down the hatches for the night? It's getting too close to dark to handle it tonight. Next. Where's the food? I'm frakkin' hungry."

"And I'm ready to game."

"Um. We don't have any games here. Sorry. Haven't really had the time to think about that down here on the border."

"Well shit. Boss, what are we gonna do tonight? It's been a couple days since we hit *Call of Duty*."

"I've got an idea. Lt.? Do you have anyone here that plays D&D or the equivalent?"

"Actually, I used to. And I think a few of my guys do on their downtime."

"Well, let's get our grub on and kill some imaginary orcs, trolls, and whatever other sort of despicable beings we can throw together." Bert was indeed intrigued on what they could come up with. This should be fun.

Chapter 13

Monday, October 28th

The Apache and Cobra both did a quick fly-by of the McAllen Reserve station. Devastation was all they could see for at least a mile in every direction. Bodies littered the entire area; zombies, civilians, and military alike. Both choppers hovered over the area much slower while Tommy called back to the Harlingen base with an update.

"Cobra One to Hooker One. Cobra One to Hooker One."

"You know I really hate that call sign, right?"

"It's either that or ChiCom One. Way too Commie for me to call an American. What else should we call a Chinook?"

"You suck, Tommy. You know that? What do you got?"

"Everyone here is dead. There are literally a hundred or more bodies all over the area. This was a hell of a firefight. A bunch of civilians lost their lives here too. Unknown from up here if they were on our side or not. Whatever happened, zombies invaded en masse. Let me know what the Major wants to do. Standing by."

"Copy that. Be right back." Muttonchop jumped out of the helicopter and walked over to Bert. It took a couple minutes and then Bert jumped on.

"Hey Tommy. Bert here. Can you see anyone alive?"

"No sir. Nothing but bodies. For about a square mile and more. Fencing torn down in spots and one of the front gates is gone. Might be evidence of the buildings in the compound broken into but I really can't see from up here." After a second, he added, "At least no one is taking shots at me this time."

"C'mon back then. No use in wasting fuel. I'll send a couple Humvees to check it out. There could be some useful items there still. See you in a few."

"Copy that boss."

The small convoy slowed to a crawl as they neared the base. There was only so far they could drive without rolling over corpses. Something they didn't need to do; except in the direst of circumstances. Still fifty yards away from the entrance, they stopped and disembarked. Weapons at the ready, they searched the entire area for any survivors.

Branching out, they went in groups of two all the way around the compound until they met up on the backside. Radioing the rest, everyone moved into base and searched it too. Most of the doors were wide open and items were scattered everywhere. It didn't look as if things were ransacked; more like the men had scrambled to keep resupplying themselves. Bullets and guns were all over the shelves and floor in disarray. It would take a while to pick it all up and figure out what the many pieces are. Some were actually in pieces. When the shit hit the fan, someone had been cleaning and reassembling some of the guns.

"Rover Team to Reserve One. Come in Reserve One."

"Go for Reserve One."

"Giant mess on the ground here. No survivors. Seems there was a major fight to stay alive and they lost. No obvious bad guys present. Just looks like they got overrun by a giant wave of infected. Couldn't be more than two days since it happened. Advise."

"Stand by." The radio operator at the Harlingen base ran over to the brass. Bert and the lieutenant walked to the radio.

"Rover Team, this is Major Bharata. I hear there are no survivors, correct?"

"Correct, sir."

"All right. How about ordinance? Anything recoverable?"

"Yes sir. Quite a lot sir. It's just scattered everywhere."

"Do your best to grab everything. Watch your back though. Set up guards. I don't want to lose any of you over a few weapons. Copy?"

"Yes sir. We will have to move a bunch of bodies though sir. Could take a while. We can't drive near the compound yet."

"Do what you have to but get back here before sundown. That's an order. As much of an order as I will give anyway."

"Still an order to us sir. I was hoping maybe we can do a quick search of the area also sir. Maybe find some survivors somewhere holed up. I can't see everyone being dead in the area."

"Sounds good, soldier, but the order still stands. Make it back here before sundown."

"Aye, aye, sir. We're on it. Over and out."

The men dutifully picked up and moved bodies for over an hour. Those that started to get tired would take over guard duty and this rotation would continue till they could bring in the vehicles. The sergeant in charge directed most of them to pile up all the ordinance they could. Leave anything that might be damaged if space was limited. A few others would continue to keep watch.

No incidents occurred during the load-up. Afterwards, they moved around the neighborhood areas with still plenty of daylight left. Every once in a while, the sergeant would call out over the loudspeaker hooked up to the radio. Their intentions were to draw out anyone that wanted help. What they got was a buttload of biters when they rounded a large street corner.

There had to be a very large pack of immeasurable numbers right on the main street. Many were tearing apart what used to be citizens, animals, and even some of their own. Between the loudspeaker and the trucks screeching to a halt, a few dozen looked up, screeched and howled, then it was on. Fresh meat was in the air and it was almost dinner time. The sergeant told the Humvee behind him to back it up quickly and his truck did the same.

One of his men opened up with the big M2 .50 caliber on the roof while several other guns were firing from open windows. Full gear backwards with extremely loud firepower was the order of the day. Body parts went flying all over while many more started heading their way. Only a few stopped to munch on their comrades while the majority stepped around or on them to get to the meat in uniforms.

"Watch the left! They're coming down the alleys, too! Shit!" There was nowhere to turn around yet. Each time they got to an opening in-between the buildings, munchers were already coming at them. This group was much larger than they originally saw. The loudspeaker, obvious now, had not been a good idea. It had drawn all within earshot running. It was the dinner bell and shit just got real.

It was four blocks back before the tail Humvee broke through into a large enough space to turn around. It spun to face back towards the Reserve compound and set up shop. The lead Humvee's M2 was red hot by this time after a second reload. As soon as it went past the tail to turn, the second opened up on the ensuing mob heading their way. It seemed as if the whole of

McAllen was riding their ass looking for the beef. Zombie after zombie went down with no end in sight. The front truck got spun around and took off. The munchers just got to the tail Humvee when they were able to move again. One of the men had his arm grabbed before he could reel it back inside. Yelling and punching in terror for his life he couldn't get a shot off. The man in the front seat reached back and put a knife in the zombie's head.

"Shit! Shit! Shit! Am I bit? Did it get me?" The guy in the back seat was panicking.

"Chill out, brother. You got away. One more dead zombie and we lost no one. You're all good." The two-truck caravan was off and moving. The M2 lit up a few more that had come out of the side roads as they went by and then went silent.

"We're clear."

The sergeant came over the radio. "Everyone okay back there?"

"All good, sir. Peterson almost lost his arm, but Jackson put a knife in the Z's head."

"Thank God. That was a good job boys. Planning couldn't have made that go any better. Let's get the hell back to Harlingen."

Keying the radio to another channel, he spoke again. "Reserve One, this is Rover Team. Come in."

"Go for Reserve One."

"Heading back now. Ran into a swarm trying to find others. None found alive. Also have a boatload of armaments."

"Anyone down, Rover Team?"

"All good. No bites. Close though. It felt like we ran into the whole town at once. I would suggest avoiding McAllen anytime soon. It's gone; not one survivor found."

"Copy that. Saying a prayer for all of them. Go ahead and pick the area clean on the way. Plenty of daylight to stock up in. C'ya in an hour or so then. Stay safe."

"Roger. Over and out." Hitting the highway, they picked up the pace and said their own prayers. Too many people dying, and no one knew why yet. Such a giant waste of homo sapiens.

Chapter 14

After Breakfast, Lake Jackson

Construction began again on the neighborhood fence line once everyone was finished eating. Aaron, Wayne, Jose, Danny, and Kylar all went out together for supplies. Michael had made the executive decision that only people his boys knew and trusted explicitly would go out with them. He didn't want them to go through a similar problem to yesterday. Turns out that Ron and Bill had been lovers for several years now. This explained what happened. At least part of it. Maybe Bill couldn't handle losing Ron. They might never know. Emotions can run very high when a loved one dies. Some people just don't come back from that.

Turns out the girls wanted to go out this time too. Both of William's daughters, Haley and Holley, wanted to go with the younger boys but he was having none of that. They were too young to be out there without an actual need to be. Wayne had been flirting with the older of the two for a few months before the apocalypse. Wayne being sixteen and Haley only a month from the same; with Holley two years her younger. It would take some time and training before William would even think about letting his daughters out from under his thumb. A lot of time. William's primary job being to protect his little girls. Shelter them for as long as possible. Without the little ladies, they still had plenty of help. Having eight people going though allowed for them to take four pickup trucks along with trailers. Each vehicle could have a gunner if needed too. Their group was gone within thirty minutes of eating. The plan was to move even further out than the past.

The convoy moved out slowly, slugging up to the gate and then slowly moving through the neighborhood. A few random zombies became road pancakes from the large dually that Aaron drove. It didn't matter if they felt Aaron was a threat, were hungry, or if they just wanted to die; obliged they would be. A couple thumps here, a few more speedbumps there and they were out onto Highway 288 South.

They rolled along at a decent pace until they got near the plant entrance before going into Freeport. Aaron stopped and waited for the others to pull alongside. It was a large highway with plenty of room for them all. And it wasn't like someone was going to come flying up behind them. Lately they had been wondering how many more people they might actually find alive down here. New faces were scarce.

"Dude, what's up?" Kylar was first over to the big truck.

"Look out there." Aaron directed their attention out over the massive amount of land the plants were sprawled on. "There has to be a couple thousand plus."

"Holy shit! They're everywhere. But they are just walking. Where are they going?" Wayne had an inquisitive mind.

"Let me call dad. He might know something." Aaron picked up his phone and dialed. Cells were still working but it was only a matter of days now before they were completely gone. The signal was frizzing with robotic sounds as it cut in and out.

"Dad. Dad! Can you hear me?"

"…hear you…you okay?"

"I'll hit you on the radio, dad. Cell signal is starting to cut out."

"Give…minute." Michael walked over to the closest radio; set up on a table near the entrance to the houses. He had been helping set up more fencing.

Aaron switched over to their common channel on the CB they had installed in the truck. "Dad. Can you hear me now?"

"I'm here son. Are you okay?"

"All good dad but there's something weird going on. A few thousand zombies are walking into the plants. Not running or anything else. Just a long line of them coming from all over the area and walking into the plants."

"What the hell are they doing?"

"We were hoping you would know."

"Where are you?"

"Right now, we are sitting on top of the 288 bridge overlooking them. Nothing up here to worry about. It's almost like they don't know what the ramps are for. Don't they know they could avoid all the signal lights if they just jumped on the highway?" Danny and the others laughed as he said that.

"Funny. Just keep an eye out. Let me talk to a couple of the guys. See if we can spitball something. Keep going and I'll hit you back."

"All right, dad. We're gone." He got the others to load up and they continued on.

A few more miles down the road, they were into Freeport. Not the best looking of towns but lots of appeal to those looking for things to do. Plenty of history in this fishing town. A few infected stood around here and there. Some eating out of the trash, some ran from the vehicles, a few stared at them as they drove past, and one tried to run toward them. The feverhead was hobbled with a leg injury and just ended up looking silly. They were past him pretty quick and watched as he got distracted by something else shortly thereafter. Kind of like a dog. *Squirrel!*

"Hey, Aaron. Stop up ahead at that Buccee's. We should try and get some coolers full of ice and see if there are any drinks we can purloin." Using the radio, Danny had made a great suggestion but was about to regret his word choice.

"Purloin? What the heck is that? Are you a frakkin' high and mighty intellectual now?" Jose was the first to take a shot.

"Why, yes. I am an intellectual. I do have a degree."

"Whoopidy do. I bet you hold your pinky finger in the air when you drink your tea, too." Kylar's turn.

"Hardy, har, har. You people are hilarious. Just pull it over, brain fart."

"Yes sir. Don't want to upset our overlord, now do we? Everybody pull over. He might start throwing a temper tantrum. Someone get him a box of crayons and some construction paper. We'll find him a safe space, so he doesn't get too offended by us." Everyone was laughing now. Even Danny.

"Oh, my God. Shut the hell up. You're killing me. I can't even frakkin' breath. *Safe space.* That shit was so stupid." Danny was trying to drive through the tears.

All along the road, infected were seen but so far none of them were much interested in the convoy. Either they were full or didn't see them as a threat. Aaron pulled over into the parking lot and up to a gas pump. Might as well stay topped off. Each of the guys jumped out and made a ready weapons check. No sense in being caught unawares. A few of them went up to the doors and looked inside for any signs of a problem. Ransacked but otherwise zombie free.

Jose went behind the counter to set the pumps up. Electricity helped while it was still on. It would be a much larger issue when that went out. Might have to suck out the gas from the tanks themselves. Once that was done, he ran back outside to help the others fill up. Wayne stayed outside to stand guard while Aaron was filtering through the store. The front aisle yielded some sodas, automobile fluids, and other accessories but the next was a goldmine of candy and chips. He gathered what he could while some of the others started toward the cooler. Just as the first person rounded the corner a loud 'Shit!' rang out.

"What the hell was that?" Kylar had hit his ass on the floor while trying to scramble backwards and Aaron was working his way toward him.

"A gigantic rat. That's what. Damn bear of a raccoon. He ran around the other end. I'm not sure who was scared more. Help my ass up." Kylar was embarrassed but no harm was done.

"Are y'all okay in there? I thought I heard a—Shit! Holy crap that thing was huge." Danny was near the front of the store when the raccoon ran out. "That was a horse. I pity the Z that tries to eat that one. Probably end up as dinner itself."

"Guys. Let's get the ice, drinks, and whatever else we can use. We're wasting time." Aaron was laughing but knew he had to keep everyone moving. He was still three months from his eighteenth birthday, but you have to become a man really fast when you live among the zombies. They got the trucks going again within ten minutes. There were still a couple small lumber stores in the area to hit up.

After a few trips, they made it back to Lake Jackson with a pretty big final load. This time they took it over to the Wal-Mart. They needed some of the barb wire found so they could line the animal pen. It would help them take down any infected that got that close. Slow them up some. Odds are they would never make it that far unless there were too many to shoot from a distance. Barb wire can be a great equalizer.

"Hey, boys. Have you seen our new toys out front?" Warren started to walk them through the store.

"Toys? Did you find another helicopter?" Wayne perked up.

"Just wait." They made it out the front, warily. Aaron and Wayne just stood there gaping.

"Tanks? You got frikkin' tanks? I've got to drive one someday." Wayne, still a teenager at heart, unlike his brother, ran up to them and climbed around. Aaron walked over calmly and climbed up onto the same trailer. After a few minutes of geeking out, they started to climb down, then walked back towards the store with Warren.

While the boys were tank gawking, their father radioed. Them being in front and the radios behind the store, they hadn't heard.

"Aaron or Wayne. Come in." Michael waited a second and radioed again. "Aaron or Wayne. Come in. Is there anyone manning the radio?"

"Danny here. Is this Michael?"

"Yeah. Hey, bud. I got a job for y'all if you're up for it. Where are you right now?"

"Posted up at Wally's. Unloading."

"Okay. That's good. You can still do this."

"Lay it on me."

"You don't have time for another run down there for supplies, but you do have time to return to the area with sunlight remaining. I'm hoping you can stay the night down there. Maybe grab more stuff tomorrow. Thinking you could take a look down near the beaches for us. We're gonna need to fish soon. Quickest route is the Quintana or Surfside beaches or even the Freeport docks. Also thinking you could take a look at the local ships. There has to be at least one fishing trawler still there. I know Captain Elliot used to run from there."

"Good idea. We'll pack what we need for camping while we're here. I'll see how many volunteers I can get. Maybe we can stay at a beach house."

"I really hope you find someone alive down there. I don't know of any of us that can run a fishing boat. One way or the other we will get one in the water. Don't really have a choice in that."

"On it, boss. We'll keep in touch. Out." Danny signed off and walked inside to Aaron and the others.

"Hey. Bossman has a job for us."

"Bossman? You mean dad? I doubt he would like being called that. I don't think he likes being in charge either." Wayne was heaving a roll of wire over to the closest part of the fence line with Kylar. The ladies and others were all moving wood and smaller supplies off the trucks.

"He's the man making the right decisions though. Everyone is looking to him. Even William, Steve, and Davis are taking cues from him too." Danny moved to help them with the big roll.

"Yeah. Dad was always good at making the right calls. Except when it came to his costumes for the comic cons. God. He once went in a Pikachu onesie with a Chewbacca mask, bandolier belt, and a little six-inch crossbow that shot water pellets. Called himself PikaChewie. Funny as hell but the onesie was a little too tight. It looked so bad, but he didn't care. People took pictures with him though, so I don't know how bad the decision was after all. He even got a five second shot on the WB news report on the con that night." Aaron was recalling last year's Comicpalooza in Houston.

"Let's get this shit unloaded. I want as much daylight as we can get. And thanks for that very vivid and disturbing picture that is now burned in my head." Jose had a practical mind and realized it might take time to get enough done just today. And you never knew what could happen tomorrow. Not nowadays anyway.

Chapter 15

South Texas Division

"Bert to Timmons's farm, come in." Waiting a minute, he started again. "Bert to Timmons's farm, someone come in."

"Hey, Bert. This is Patrick. How can I help?"

"Howdy do Patrick. Just wanted to let y'all know that a few of us will be stopping by to stay the night and check things out. Don't go to any trouble to accommodate though. We'll make do."

"No trouble at all. We have extra tents and dinner will be ready in an hour or so. I'll let Georgia Hall know. She has taken to doing the majority of the cooking for us."

"Good. I bet you're eating great then. About eight of us are staying and the rest will be heading on to the base. We'll set down away from the ranch. Don't wanna spook the horses or bring any unfriendlies to you."

"Appreciate it, sir. See you in a while."

"Copy that. Out."

Muttonchop set the Chinook down about a hundred yards out from the farmhouse with grace and a very small bump of a landing. Grateful, they all popped out and headed toward the home except for Papa and Jim Lee. They waited till Mutt was done shutting the engine down. They saw only two infected anywhere close, but they stayed well away from them. Jim wasn't sure if it was because of fear or a proper sense of instinct. Maybe even an instinctual fear of a higher form of predators in their midst. A bigger badder animal they needed to avoid. Whatever. Once Mutt was out they moved off together.

Beers had been handed out already by the time they came inside, so they partook and joined the crowed porch out back. A lot of patted backs and hand shaking went around; it had been a week since some of them had seen each other. Once they were all settled, a young man of fifteen years came and hugged Bert.

"Thank you, sir. You saved my life last week."

"Morgan Grimes, right?" Morgan nodded his head yes. "It is such a miracle seeing you walking and talking. Much less in what great condition you are in. You look like you've gained a little weight but not fat."

"Yes, sir. I've been working outside a lot. I think I even lost a few more pounds of fat and I feel great. I don't know about the gaining though. Maybe you just saw me at a bad time. The bite is just a scar already. I miss Billy though. He was my friend since first grade."

"I wish I could have gotten to you faster Morgan. Another senseless tragedy. I'm sorry for the loss of your friend, too. Scared me to death when I saw you get bitten but I am certainly thankful to God that you somehow survived."

"Well, sir. I'll let you get back to your meeting. I just wanted to come by and thank you. If I can ever help, please tell me. I know I'm young, but I want to learn from Mr. Dupree and the others when I can."

"We would be happy to start training you on certain things if you are ready? I can show a few of you how to handle firearms tomorrow; while I'm here. You're old enough to learn how to shoot." After a thoughtful second though, he said, "Do I need to ask permission from anyone first?"

"No, sir. My parents are probably gone. I know this. If they are still alive, I have no way to find them. They weren't answering their cell phones when I tried the first few days. I can only hope and pray, sir. All of you are now my parents."

"I'm sorry, Morgan. That has to be hard. I know it doesn't help but I can't get ahold of my parents either." Vinny put a hand on the boy's shoulder in comfort. "So, other adults here? What say you of my training this fine young man?"

A ring of yes's and hell yes's went around the porch area with smiles to boot. "Then let's do this."

"That would be great, sir. What time do you want me ready? I know you have to head back sometime tomorrow."

"Let's get a good early start. Right after sunup. Say seven. That should give everyone time to eat and it will be bright enough. Give us a few hours of teaching. I'm sure there are a few others that could use it besides you. Spread the word for me."

"You got it, sir. Thank you." With that, Morgan was off with a huge smile.

"That boy has a lot of potential. I'm still curious on the virus though. It has to have done something to his system. He really does look bigger and more fit than before. Is it just me?" Bert turned to the others.

"No, sir. You're right. Something in him has changed. He's even become more of a man already mentally on top of his changed appearance. He hardly even plays with the other kids anymore. Morgan is always wanting to help somewhere. Working with the fencing, horses, or even just mucking the stalls when needed. It's as if he feels that his childhood is over already. Kind of worried about him." Mr. Paul Timmons, owner of the property, had been the one guiding young Morgan the last few days. Teaching him how to work the ranch and basically adopting the little man.

"That's what I thought. He even carries himself in a manly way compared to last week. We need someone to talk with him. Maybe you can, Ms. Sharpe?" Bert turned to the former principal.

"I certainly can. I will try tomorrow after your exercise is done Vincent."

"Please call me Vinny."

"Um, Bert. I can help too. We never got to talk about it, but I was a psychologist before all of this. Maybe I can feel him out and see if there is something wrong or if he has just decided to grow up more quickly."

"Wow. Thank you, Randall. That's a surprise. I guess maybe we ought to find out what everyone's specialties are, huh? I never would have thought to ask. Never hurts though, right? Well, then. Morgan is in good hands. I might add that maybe you should talk to all the kids at some point. There's no telling how each is taking this new world. I know almost all of them no longer have parents."

"I might add that I talk to each adult also. The toll of everyone's loss has to be thought of. Even those adults that think they don't need me. Maybe I can just have casual conversations. That includes you, Bert."

"I don't think I need it, but I do see how you're right. I will reluctantly give in and talk too. But. It will have to wait a few days. Too much going on. Maybe after Halloween. Speaking of which. Has anyone discussed the night?"

"We're going to throw something together here, but we need to run out for candy and costumes. Hasn't been much time for that stuff." John Stockton, original member of the hospital crew chimed in. "My son, Tim and his girlfriend were going to go out with a few others and see what they could find. Stores should be full of Halloween stuff."

"Sounds good. I'll see if we can get a few more from the air station to help with that if Tonia can spare some. We'll bring over the children too that night. Might as well get everyone involved.

Maybe a crew or two could go on a special mission. Will do people good to have something to look forward to."

"Hey, Bert. I have a request, too." Jeffrey Hall, parent rescued from the first school, kind of raised his hand in partial embarrassment. "Sir. I know you probably have all the pilots you need over there but... I would like to learn as much as I can. Even if I never get off the ground because of fuel or need. The thing I would like the most is to train on the mechanics of whatever is there. The opportunity was never there for me before, so I'd like to take advantage of the lack of educated people available now."

Bert stared at him dumbfounded. This brave big man rarely spoke and had really proven himself when they needed him to get that bus moving before. It had never occurred to him to train people on things until today. First Morgan with wanting to learn and now Jeff.

"Well, hell yes. That would be a great idea. This world could always use another to keep things running and I think it would be a good idea to have all the pilots we can muster. Like you said; don't know how long fuel will last but why not learn everything you could, right? How about you and yours move back to the base the day after the party. Damn good idea."

After another minute, Bert spoke again. "You know guys. Maybe we need to start a second list to go with the known specialties. This one to find out what people want to learn along the way. Backups are never a bad thing in all aspects. With that in mind, Vinny, maybe you ought to feel out as many as possible for ops. With only three of you with major operations training, it would be a real good idea to start training more."

"Yes, sir. I agree and have been thinking on that. Already, several at the base have proven themselves ready to rise to the next level. I have a list started just for that reason."

"Once again you're ahead of me. Good."

"I have one other thing we need to discuss before we head for dinner, sir."

"Shoot, Vinny."

"I think we need to consider hitting a hospital or two real soon. Supplies will get scarce if we run into any big trouble and I sure don't want some gangbanger or cartel piss-ant getting to the goods first."

"Good call. I'm afraid my old stomping grounds were overrun when we left. But. That means that it probably hasn't been raided either. There was a massive amount of infected running through the corridors. Maybe don't start there but it should be a goldmine of meds. When we get back tomorrow, we'll drum up some volunteers. I think I'll get on the horn with Michael and John about that same thing. It would be a good idea for anybody listening on the radio to try and do that same thing."

"If you okay it; me, Papa, and Jim Lee will take the Medical Center. Let some other crews do the same for some of the other hospitals. We should take the hardest loads until we get more volunteers trained. Maybe you, Rosa, and Don could get a good list of things for us to gather. Grab everything else we can pack after that."

"We'll work on that for you. All right people. I need another beer and I'm hungry. Let's grub."

Chapter 16

Beach Excursion

"Hey guys. Mind if I tag along? I'll bring my SUV, too. I used to work with someone that lives down on Surfside Beach. Go fishing with him every once in a while. He might even know how to drive one of those boats. I've been getting a little worried about him and his family. I haven't been able to get ahold of him since this all started." Warren was helping them find some pillows and blankets for the night out.

"I don't see why not. We could use someone to navigate the waters. The more the merrier. Is your wife coming, too?" Aaron had always liked Warren. He had the same strange sense of humor his dad had, an older geek, too.

"No. She's staying behind. It seems that she has found her calling here at Wal-Mart. Getting up in the morning and cooking for everyone gets her juices flowing. Taking care of people seems to be her new lot in life and she is loving it."

"Okay. We'll put you in the middle of the pack. At least this way, if shooting needs to be done, you'll have cover on either side."

"Thanks. Kind of hard to shoot and steer unless your Mad Max or John Wick." Sam lightly punched Aaron on the arm and they got moving.

Aaron and Kylar were rolling down Quintana beach slowly and carefully, needing to see if there were any survivors along this part of the coast. It was a decent size area with RV campsites, cabins, and a meeting house. The others were all driving along the roadway, so they could check out the houses on the waterfront.

Amazingly, no bodies were seen anywhere. No infected, no half-eaten civilians, no nothing. In the short distance, they could see the large meeting house that used to be reserved for parties and the like. When they got within fifty yards, a few people stepped out and raised some rifles. Aaron immediately stopped while Wayne handed him a gun, just in case. This was definitely not what they expected.

"Who are you and what do you want!?" A taller man in the group in front of them yelled out.

"Don't shoot." Kylar took it upon himself to hop out, knowing that Aaron was about to. No need for the young man to be in a direct line of fire. Once Kylar was out, he moved to the front of Aaron's truck. Not in his sightline but so that he was the man's focus instead.

"We're just looking for other survivors. Not here to harm or intrude." Kylar was a little nervous but he knew if one of Michael's sons got hurt, his ass was grass.

"We've done a pretty good job of staying alive so far. Why are you looking? And who are you?"

"We're just part of a larger group in Lake Jackson. Special sense of responsibility that we have to look for more. That whole keeping the human race going thing."

This caused the man to chuckle a little. "Well. Let's meet you all. Drive behind us up to the lodge. When you get out, leave your weapons in the trucks, though. We don't know you well enough yet."

"Okay." Kylar moved back to his truck and they moved on slowly behind the walking group. Parking right up close, they left everything in the truck, but Wayne decided to stay back. No use in completely giving up. Better to be cautious. And the trucks were close enough that Wayne could hear them talking as long as they didn't go inside. Which they wouldn't. Just in case.

Introductions were made between the two groups while a few more people trickled out of the large meeting lodge. Multiple families and children could be seen running around inside as they spoke. Aaron and his band learned that as things became bad, many migrated towards the lodge because it had been the most easily defensible. Some people had been lost along the beach line when it got really bad. Seeing as the area is sparsely populated, the amount of infected was kept low though. The band of survivors had buried everyone, from zombie to civilian. This was the reason it looked so good along the beach front.

Kylar did most of the talking for the first few minutes and then introduced Aaron. This was a more natural way for them to see him as the leader. This new group was hanging on his every word as he gave them the rundown on the Wal-Mart, their new makeshift neighborhood, allies in Southwest Houston, and their new military friends. Hearing about this just made their decision to become part of the larger groups much easier. Seeing and listening to this well-mannered and articulate young man bolstered their confidence that life would get better; even during an infected landslide.

While speaking, he heard back from Jose and the rest that they had found a few more stragglers in homes by themselves. The people wanted to stay where they were; some under the impression that this would all blow over somehow. They had given them radio call numbers and even cell information. Though no one knew how long mobile phones would continue to work as they were starting to get squirrely already. Aaron told them to relay that the lodge was their next best bet if things got hairy. The rest of the group was going to head back his way as it was starting to get dark. The plan was to find a nice beach house that was no longer occupied and stay the night.

The lodge group informed them that plenty were open nearby and they were welcome to stay for dinner. Fish was the name of the game for the night. Something that was plentiful and easy to get where they were. Now that they were looking towards the ocean, several boats were moored up along the shoreline and the dock that headed out nearby. The dock held some of the bigger boats for deeper fishing. Over the next few days, they could begin to trade with Lake Jackson for some vegetables and vice versa with the fish. Mutually beneficial to all. The new people were quite happy to have been stumbled upon. Once Jose, Danny, and Warren got there, beer was handed out.

The one thing that had not been relayed was the incredible find they had ran across. A small store was set up about a mile from there and had been basically abandoned in the aftermath. Raiding had commenced. They brought back all the beer and wine the little store had. Along with whatever food was still good and bags of ice. The lodge group had only let a few people venture that far over the last week and they had left quite a lot behind; since they hadn't taken a vehicle and only a four-wheeler that had finally run out of gas. Having vehicles to carry gave Jose and the others a gigantic leg up on ransacking.

Wayne radioed Michael and let him know what and who they had found for the night. Elated, he told him to inform them that he looked forward to meeting their new group members. Hopefully the next day. The boys would proceed to Surfside Beach tomorrow; wanting to make it as far as the Blue Water Highway that ran to Galveston. They still had to look near the Freeport docks at whatever fishing boats might still be there. After signing off with his dad, he went inside with the others, now all content to have gotten better acquainted. From here, they proceeded to have a great night getting to know each other better. And a lot of story swapping.

Chapter 17

Tuesday, October 29th

The boys awoke to a wonderful but weird smell. Fish for breakfast. It had been a while since they had fish, not counting the night before, but for breakfast? Oh, well. When in Rome, do as the Romans do. Having as many in the lodge as they did, the whole group had been settled into one room for the night. Each of them got up slowly to the same smell. They gathered themselves and proceeded downstairs. Greeted heartedly before the first foot hit the base of the stairs.

"Good morning. Did y'all have a good sleep? The lot of you stayed up a while playing from what I heard. My old ass was out by nine. I just can't do the late-night thing anymore." Justin was the older man that had greeted them the night before.

"Sometimes I think I'm already getting too old myself. And I'm only seventeen. Been a lot of late nights this past week. Oh well. I guess we'll all sleep when we're dead, right?" Aaron was carrying a lot of weight on his young shoulders lately.

"So cynical for someone so young but I would say it's to be expected. Everyone come and find a seat somewhere. Most have already eaten. The kids seem to get up early and it forces their parents to rise with them. I'll get y'all fixed up."

Throughout breakfast, they relayed their agenda. Aaron told of their plan to recon Surfside next for survivors and then they could circle back to refuel them enough to get to Lake Jackson to meet the group. Justin was looking forward to meeting everyone and seeing how they could all help each other. Once they were done eating, they hurriedly moved out of the lodge. The area northeast of Highway 332 went all the way to Galveston. That was too much for them to do alone. Moving slowly, it would take almost half the day to secure this side of Surfside. If there wasn't an infected landslide awaiting them. Only time would tell. But first they had to get moving. Conserving fuel since they weren't going to be hauling anything, they left all but two trucks behind, unhooking the trailers for fast travel in case it was needed. Then they were gone.

Loaded up with two in the front and one in the back as a gunner of each truck, the three ladies left behind, the boys were rolling past the Quintana/Surfside line. There was nothing seen for a while but then some of the road started to be partially blocked here and there from vehicles and just a few bodies. Surfside didn't have the same clean-up crew as Quintana did. Preparing for the worst, they decided to disembark from the pickups for a while as the way was more hazardous.

Prepping all their weapons and throwing on some backpacks full of supplies, they moved out along the road. Carefully moving along, eyes on a swivel, they looked around each home and vehicle they came across. They had made it halfway down the beach road when they started hearing strange sounds from ahead. As they moved, the noise was getting louder and more distinct. It was the sound of hunger. Some howling, shrieking, and growling could be heard. They were still several houses away from whatever they were hearing but caution was best at this time. Knowing it was on the beach side, they each started fast walking around each stilt home in a row. Constantly looking backwards and all around them. Even in the stark daylight a biter could surprise them if not completely aware of their surroundings. No one wanted to get jumped like Alberto did that first day. Zombie rape was not on their agenda. EVER!

They got within two houses before they spotted where the sick and twisted sounds were coming from. There were about a dozen infected milling around a burnt-out staircase. Each house on the beach was on stilts in case of flooding so they all had stairs leading up to a front porch. This one looked as if it was firebombed and it had a steel grate of a gate at the top. No one could get up or down it. It was toast. Literally.

Whispering, Warren suggested that a couple of them try to look around the backside of the house. Nodding his approval, Aaron watched as Warren, Wayne, and Jose took off around the backside of the house they were hiding behind. They crawl-walked around and up behind the closest house. Peering around, Sam could see there was no back stair either. The same had been done as the front. Burnt to a crisp and a steel grate at the back also. The person that lived there was serious about his security. The drawback was the lack of ability to get out themselves now. They made their way back to the rest from there.

"Just as ugly in the back. Same situation with the burned staircase and a nice gate to boot. I haven't seen anyone inside yet either." Sam was giving the others the rundown.

"I think we should try to get into this next house and see what can be seen. Come up the backside. Hopefully we don't attract attention."

Then thinking, Wayne added, "If that is all right with you. Sir."

"Shut up, you ass. It's a good idea, though. We can spare a little time to check it out. We're probably going to have to take out the feverheads, but I want to make sure we don't bring too many more that we can't see yet." Aaron punched his little brother in the arm. He thought it was amazing that not too long ago they would fight each other over stupid stuff. Now they were a smooth flowing team. "Let's move slowly."

In a row again, they stalked around the back of the current house and slowly up to the back stairs of the next. Constantly looking out, they crab-walked up the stairs. Just as the last two started up, they heard a howl behind them. Two half-dressed Zs were running after them from across the street. So. There were a few more running around that weren't on food patrol at the front gate. Bringing up the rear, Jose triggered a short burst into each and ran up and into the house. Afraid the shots would bring more, they wanted to make sure they weren't seen getting inside.

As the door closed and the blinds stopped moving, Jose could see another one come up to the bodies and look around. Being hungry, the thirty-something lady started to settle down for dinner. Locking the door quietly, Jose moved away and they all went into the living room to watch the house next door.

"I think I saw something through the curtain. It looks like a man. He doesn't have blackout curtains, but he is trying to obscure himself as much as he can." Danny was taking the first watch.

After a minute or so, Kylar had an idea. "Hey. What if we threw a small rock at the side of the house. Maybe get his attention. Let him know he has help out here."

"Damn good suggestion. Do it." Aaron found a window they could open with a minimum of sound and not one the zombies were looking toward. Kylar found one of those table-top pebble things in the living room. He proceeded to throw one at the opposite wall every minute or so. Finally, part of the curtain moved aside to look. The surprise on the man's bearded face was one for the ages. Seeing someone next door was the last thing he expected.

Now they had to communicate. It was Wayne's turn to come up with an idea. He found some paper and wrote his cell phone number on it. Then he showed it to the man. Unfortunately, the man gave the cutoff gesture that he didn't have a cell. He moved away from the window and found some paper of his own. Writing on it, he told them that there was no home phone there either.

The writing went back and forth a few more times. Aaron was letting him know they would get him out of there soon. Relaying that they wanted to make sure there weren't too many more zombies running around before they mowed down those out front. Jose went back to the rear and saw that the woman was no longer there. So, they knew they had one bogey running free. Maybe more.

One last word to the beard that they were moving out and would be with him shortly and they were off. They opened the back door and walked out with weapons at the ready. As soon as they stepped foot outside, the woman was back. Jose put a shot straight through her chest. As he got down to the bottom, first in line, a second suited man came charging and howling at them. Another double-tap and he was down too. All six of them were boots on the ground when some of the front posse came charging around the corner; drawn by the gunfire. Aaron and Wayne were last in line and took down the three that ran at them. Coming up between the two houses, two more came flying toward them. Getting to be too close, it was time for hand-to-hand combat. Skylar, being the strongest, pulled out a hand axe and waded in. Shearing off the top of one skull, he hit the other in the face with his opposite elbow. Spinning, he swung the axe and buried it into the other's chest. Down and done. Skylar kept the axe in his left hand with his pistol in the right. Never know what was coming.

More than half a dozen infected were still up front with an unknown number somewhere in the vicinity. They could clearly see the rest of the zombies past the stilt pillars of the house, but they weren't interested in them yet. Slowly, they picked off each of them from where they were until all were down. Now they just had to figure out how to get the man down without stairs. They set up a half circle perimeter around the front while Aaron called out to the man.

"Sir. You can come out now. They are all down. We are watching out for more." Stepping out, they could see he was larger than anticipated. This was going to be fun.

"Hey guys. Thank you so much. I'm outta food up here. Except for chips. My name's Chandler by the way."

"Do you have any rope or anything up there? We're trying to figure out how to get you down."

"Let me look." He went back inside for a few minutes while Jose and Danny peeled off to check the house they were just at. Something they didn't think about when they were in it.

"I got a small piece up here. It's only six feet long. What do you want me to do?"

"Hold on for now. We're looking for more." Having no joy at the first house, they moved to the next and then the next. After the third and another zombie shot, they came back with some double-braided sailing rope. Eighteen feet in all. They threw it up to him and had him tie it off. Then he slowly tried to descend it with a few of them underneath to catch. He made it a couple feet down before he lost his grip and fell. Danny and Skylar caught him on the way down. Well, caught isn't exactly how it went. More like he fell on them and they all went down. A few bruised butts and shoulders but the man was safe.

"I'm sorry. My hands get sweaty way to easy. Are y'all okay?" He put his hand out to help each of them back up.

"All good, sir." Brushing himself off, Danny asked, "What happened to the stairs?"

"It wasn't my house. I was just trying to get away, but my car got stuck amongst all the others. I had to run and saw the steel gates on this one. They came up after me and I was afraid they would get through. So, I threw a couple Molotov cocktails at them. Smart at the time but kinda cornered myself in after. Poured water on the closest part so it would stop from taking down the house. Fun times, right?" He chuckled a little.

"Well, let's get moving. Danny, why don't you and Jose take Chandler back to the trucks and see if you can maneuver towards us a little. We still have some beach to check and would like a ride back instead of a long walk. Right guys?" Aaron was now playing politician in a way too.

"On it, boss. Chandler, if you will. Stay between us. We won't be going fast but please do whatever we say. Down, over, dive, whatever. Good?" Jose was a pretty good leader also.

"On you." Chandler fell in line and they moved on.

The rest of the west part of Surfside went somewhat uneventfully. At least relative to the last week anyway. A few more biters were milling around the furthest part of the beach, munching on a couple seagulls that didn't move fast enough. They probably thought people were there to feed them and became lunch themselves. Amazing how seagulls had this altruistic view of humanity when it came to food.

'*Good riddance,*' thought Wayne as they moved up the porch of the next house. '*Frikkin' rats with wings*' is how he thought of them anyway. They were still two houses away from the pack of eaters and they all knew it would be best to take them out now. No one wanted them to eventually become a problem later.

Opening the door to this particular home bombarded them with the most horrendous smell any of them had ever had the misfortune to encounter. Worse than the trash pit at the plants. Each of them had to cover their noses with their built-in gas mask. Their shirts. Aaron, Wayne, and Skylar couldn't exactly place the smell, but Warren had a pretty damn good idea. He was a EMT on the side before the fall and had encountered it before.

"Guys. Maybe y'all should stay in the living room while I check this out. I think I know what this is. You've seen enough and don't need this." Warren was trying to protect them but should have known better.

"Whatever it is, we probably should. I mean, look what all we have seen and done already. This could only be educational, right?" Aaron started to think he knew where and what was happening too. "It's a dead body, isn't it?"

"I think so. I won't stop you but fair warning that sometimes it can be a pretty gruesome sight on top of the smell. Your shirts won't help the stench."

"Well, I'm out. I'll be outside with the fresh air." Skylar was a strong young man but knew his limits.

"I think I'm with him on this one. I'm sure we'll come across more, but I'll bow out of for this." Wayne went outside too.

"I need to see. And there may be useful items inside the room. You might need help." Aaron was all in but knew he might blow chunks.

"Come to think of it, I'm glad you're staying. There might be someone or something else in there, too. I'm getting too old to fight off a strong one. I'll get the door if you'll do the sweep." Warren put his hand on the doorknob.

"Ready." Aaron had his 9mm up and sighted for anything on the other side.

Warren shoved the door open and Aaron swept the room. Nothing. His sights settled on two bodies lying on a bed side by side. An older man and his wife were dressed in their best suit and dress and had taken the murder/suicide pact. Hands held together while he had shot her and then himself. The pistol used had dropped to the floor near the head of the bed. In love, they had taken the final trip together. It wasn't as gruesome of a sight as first worried about, but the stench got the better of Aaron. He turned away just in time but still vomited all over the dresser before he could get out the door. He heaved a few more times and then went into the bathroom to wash up.

When he came back out, Warren had already gone over the room and then closed the door. Nothing useful for them. Just the couple's clothes and personal items. Best left for the dead. They gathered what they could from the kitchen that could be gathered in hand. A couple handbags found in the cabinets helped with the carrying. At each house, stuff had been dragged out and placed near the road for pickup. Every couple houses they had a stash. When they got outside, Warren told the others what was seen inside while they moved to the road.

"Why the hell would you do that? Seems like a copout to me." Wayne didn't understand the pact.

"Some can't handle the previously unheard of when it happens. Others feel too old to go through whatever it might be. This won't be the last like this that you will see as the days go on." Warren had seen a lot and was hoping he could explain it to him.

"Still seems pretty dumb. At least go out fighting. Take a few of them out for everyone else."

"I understand your thinking but try to remember that not everyone can have your attitude toward life. There were a great many depressed people out there before this happened. This probably just sent them over the edge. This couple chose how to leave and did it together."

"I guess. I still don't get it. But I kinda understand what you're saying." Wayne was still perplexed on someone wanting to go out like that.

"And don't count out the massive number of cowards that were running around the nation. Most of them probably ran right into a zombie's waiting arms. You know. Because we have to feed everyone; even a zombie. They're just de-humanized and disenfranchised. They can't help it if humanity doesn't fit in with them. We must do everything to help them re-adjust into society. Misunderstood creatures, they are." Aaron had the same amount of tact as his father. Anti-dumbass was just the way he thought.

"Oh, God. Don't start with that leftist bullshit. Please. My ears will start to bleed. I'm gonna need a safe space myself." Wayne started chuckling.

"Let's get moving. We got one more house, but I think we'll have to put down that little group over there first." Warren just wanted to get going. Still worried about his fishing friend and he was ready to get back to his wife and the safety of their new home.

"Yeah. Separate into two groups and we'll pincer them in case they charge. They'll have to split up. Make it easier on us." Aaron had a military state of mind. He had planned to join the Marines when he graduated. Currently, he was in the most realistic boot camp imaginable. Definitely a leadership driven boot.

They took off in opposite directions from the front of the house. Aaron and Wayne automatically together with Skylar and Warren taking the near side. Coming around the next house, the younger boys had moved faster to make up the extra yardage and using hand signals, they all opened fire in short bursts. No sense in wasting bullets. These were easy kills as they were all preoccupied. Once that was done, they circled back together and headed toward the road. The two beach fronts were clear of the current crop of feverheads. As they arrived back at the roadside, Danny and the others were picking up the previous stash.

"Let's get the hell out of here. We got too much more to do before we can head home." Jose was talking about the fact they still had to check out fishing ships and reload for supplies before returning to Lake Jackson and safety.

"Let's get this stuff to the lodge for all those people. They need it much more than we do and we gotta stop at that big Buccee's on the way out. They need fuel for their trucks too. Wouldn't be a bad idea to top off ourselves; fill up our gas cans and throw a few drinks down our throats." Skylar threw the last of the booty into the back of one of the trucks and jumped into the bed.

"Aaron, do we still have time to check the other part of Surfside? I wanna check on Clarence."

"Sure Sam. No problem at all. I had actually forgotten. Sorry." He turned to the others and spoke, "Me and Sam are going to hit the other side real quick. Check on a friend. Everyone can stop at Buccee's and wait for us. Have a beer."

"Hell yeah!" Jose didn't need any other incentive after the word beer came out.

"I'll go too." Wayne was sticking by his brother.

"Allright. See y'all in a while. Someone watch over Jose. I need him sober."

"Good luck with that." Jose piped up.

Chapter 18

Surfside East

Driving over had been easy. They saw some infected munching on various animals while they parked to walk onto the beach. A few infected here and there chose to eat a bullet instead of running away from the guys. Once around the first house, they could see the long dock stretching out into the sea. The other sights to be seen was completely unexpected.

Armed men were posted up on the beach while several people were staged at various intervals reeling in and throwing fishing lines out into the great brown water of the *Gulf of Yoohoo*. The other thing they noticed was that almost all of the people were black. Not that it mattered but to only see one white man on the pier was astounding. Warren saw his friend about halfway down the pier and smiled. They walked up to the guards slowly; weapons pointed at the ground but toward them.

"Howdy do. My name is Warren. This is Aaron and Wayne. I'm here to see my good friend, Clarence."

"Wait here." One of the guard walked up the pier and got Clarence. After a few minutes, a big man with a sour face came over to them.

"What the hell do you want, white man?!"

"To see what my brother is up to, of course." Warren still had a big grin on his face.

"Well, damn. I guess I have to accept you then, huh?" Clarence dropped the charade and shook Warren's hand. "Damn good to see you still alive. I had no way to contact you. Everything went to hell so fast, I lost my cell. Like many others, that was the last thing on my mind."

"All good. I'm really happy to see you alive too. And with a lot of others. But, I gotta ask. What's with the one white guy? Is this a reverse clan rally and you're gonna string him up later?" The two guards looked back in shock; looking like they would grab Warren up in a second and start beating him to death.

"Oh, that one. Yeah. My sister married him and won't let us use him for bait."

"Bait?" The smiles on both of their faces seemed to passivate the guards a little; realizing this was part of their friendship.

"Sure. We use the bigger white men for shark bait, little ones for fish near the pier, and we make the younger guys run. You know. So, it takes away the infected. Makes less work for us and they don't come back."

This cracked Warren up. After a few seconds, he continued. "So. Just a minute. I'm still trying to catch my breath. Okay. What about the women?"

"Oh, them bitches doing our laundry and cooking our food. They is good little house crackers." Even Clarence couldn't help himself from laughing after he said that.

"Oh my God. You're killing me. I missed hanging with you." They hugged a good hello to each other and got a hold of themselves after that exchange. Even the guards were snickering. It seemed Warren and Clarence had a strange relationship of telling racist things to each other but always knowing it was in jest. No color issues between them at all. They each realized the world had been full of whiny little girls that couldn't joke anymore.

"So. Seriously. That's your brother-in-law?"

"Yeah. My wife loves him like there's no tomorrow. I really like him too. Smart man. He worked out at NASA. Decided not to go into work last Monday. Thank God. I don't believe he would have come back. Good fisher too. They have a teenage son and he used to take him hunting and camping occasionally. Not your typical nerd."

"Okay. But that doesn't explain there not being any other white people."

"Just haven't been any. We've only seen a couple since this all began, and they were leaving. In a hurry, I might add. Said something about trying to make it to Louisiana to meet up with family. Pretty sure we'll never hear from them again."

"Yeah. That's a good bet. None of us travel without at least a group of three. As you can see."

"Us?"

"Oh, sorry. Let me introduce you to these two young men. This is Aaron and Wayne. Sons of a man I worked with. Michael runs things for us in Lake Jackson."

"Howdy do, sir." "Nice to meet you." Aaron and then Wayne shook his hand.

"Good to meet you two also. Even under these circumstances. Now, Sam. What's this us you refer to?"

"We have a rather large contingent in Lake Jackson. So far three blocks of one of the neighborhoods is fenced in to live and I run the Wal-Mart up there. Staging area for helicopters and tanks."

If Clarence had been drinking something, he would have done a spit-take. "Tanks?! And you said helicopters? Seriously. You people have been busy. How many souls do you have?"

"Over one hundred and counting. The tanks were left up near the Beltway. We had to run to Pearland and gathered more people. We currently have one medical helicopter but had a few visitors recently. A large group from Corpus came up. Heavy military presence. Good bunch of people. A lot of them stayed behind to help out here."

Clarence whistled. "Damn. Would it be a problem if we rolled up there soon to meet y'all?"

"Hell no. I'll drop your name where it matters. Do you have a radio?"

"We have CB in one of the pickups. That's it."

"All right. I'll give you the channels. Just let them know when you're heading that way. Give them a heads up. Just in case. I would suggest one of you come over to Quintana with us though. Found a group over there that y'all could get with. Maybe help each other out when needed. They are holed up in the lodge over there. Keeping their beach pretty clean of Zs also."

"Really. Yeah. Let me go tell everyone else. My wife might want to go too. Be right back." Clarence walked back along the pier and gathered all he could that didn't currently have a rod and reel in the water. After a few minutes of information dissemination, he came back. Like he said, his wife was with him.

"Howdy, Warren Good to see you again."

"Trish. Always a pleasure."

"Clarence gave us a brief rundown. So, we've got neighbors and you have a big militia trying to take over the world. 'Bout right?"

"Something like that. I can fill you in on the way if you're riding with us."

Clarence spoke up. "We're gonna take our own truck. We'll need to come back tonight and I figure you have things still to do today, right?"

"Yeah. Yeah, we do. A lot actually. Good call. Well, let's get moving. Aaron, you ready?"

"Sure. And it's nice to meet you ma'am. This is my brother Wayne. Someone forgot to introduce us."

"A well-mannered young man. A pleasure to meet you too." She shook both their hands and Wayne said "Hello."

"Now we can go." Warren mussed Aaron's hair, realizing he had forgotten about the boys.

Their two-truck caravan met up with the rest at Buccee's and jumped out. Always gas up when possible. The boys ran into the rest rooms while Warren and Clarence filled up. Some of the others were milling about outside and came over to meet the new recruits. Introductions went around, as well as a few beers. Screw open container laws. This was the 'Murica. The only law now was morality and 'live'.

After everyone was ready, they drove back to the lodge. Even more introductions, talking, laughing, and the occasional serious conversation were had. Time was flowing, so after only thirty minutes, Aaron broke in.

"Guys, we need to go. Still have things to do today."

"You're right. Sorry, Clarence, but he's right. We need to look for a fishing ship and then hit another hardware store."

"No problem, old friend. We're going to stick around a little longer and talk to these fine people, then go back ourselves. I'll get with you when we are heading up your way."

"Good deal. See you later." They shook hands and the Lake Jackson crew all loaded up, along with a few extras from the lodge.

"What's the plan, oh fearless leader." Jose took a swig of beer and smiled.

"First of all, pfft." Aaron spluttered at him. "Drive up to where Captain Elliot is supposed to be docked, hit Lake Hardware, and then head back. With this many people we should be able to load up quickly and move on." Everyone nodded and jumped in their respective vehicles.

"Head 'em up. Move 'em out. Rawhide!" Wayne yelled from the back of Aaron's truck.

"You're such a dork. That show is so old." Aaron just hung his head in shame.

Chapter 19

Still in the Freeport Area

Aaron and the others started towards the middle of Freeport. Two trucks from the lodge, including Justin, followed them as they were heading home afterwards. Taking FM 1495, they turned left onto W. Brazos St. and stopped. Dozens and dozens of infected were seen along the Freeport shipping lane. It wasn't a large part of the ocean harbor, but they had some medium size ships that came through back in the day.

The infected were trying to get to all the birds along the shore and even some of the fish. Being as these were still human infected and not undead, they didn't have a problem going into the water. Some of them drown but that didn't stop most of them. Seeing the only way to the boats this way was to go right through them, he signaled everyone to back up. There was no telling how many more couldn't be seen. Aaron decided to have them go the longer way around and through more of the town; going on up 1495, left on Old Surfside Road and then left again on N. Velasco.

He had a plan to try and see if Captain Elliot's might be in dock. If not, they would continue back down the line and find another boat. They needed two in case one broke down on them, but they weren't real optimistic.

Bodies and infected were scattered all around the neighborhoods but none got near them. One became a hood ornament, another few watched them along the way, and still two more took off when they came into view. They came down N. Velasco and saw Captain Elliot's boat sitting near the dock. It was parked off and away from the dock so the infected couldn't get onto it. They could see a couple people moving around on the boat, toting guns. Just on a whim, Aaron had the idea to try to call them. Hopefully, the phones still worked.

It rang a few times before someone picked it up. "Captain Elli—Shit. Got so used to that. Who are you and what do you want?"

"Sir. My name is Aaron. You should be able to see me on the bridge in front of you. We didn't want to come over just yet. Figured we'd see if someone was on board first."

"Damn, son. You look pretty young. Are you in charge of your little caravan?"

"Yes, sir. The apocalypse makes for strange situations. I'm not the main man but I am running this mission."

"If you want, take that little boat over there near the other side and saddle up to us so we can talk. I would suggest everyone else be on the lookout though. You can bring one more with you if you want."

"Be there in a minute." He hung up his cell phone and told the others what the deal was. Wayne would go with him. Back to back the brothers would stand everywhere from now on.

Stepping off the little two-man boat, a hand reached out and helped them up one at a time. "Welcome aboard. I'm Casey. My crewmate is Elliot. No relation. The original good captain had to sell a few years back. We're all that's left."

"I'm Aaron and this is my brother Wayne. It's good to meet you."

"Howdy do to you two. Had two more with us several days ago. I guess right after the bottom dropped. We were out at sea for a three-day jaunt for fish. Lost a few other crewmates when we came back in from sea. Didn't know what was going on till it was too late. They stepped off and into sudden hell from a small group of them. We barely got pushed back off and a few of them dropped into the water and drowned."

"Glad you made it, then. Probably a lot of people died not knowing what was going on. We kind of saw some of it in the news and even more on the net before it all went to hell. Problem was most watch the main local media and never heard a thing. They weren't prepared."

"We sure as hell weren't. Don't have a lot of time to watch TV when you have to fish for a living and the seasons keep getting shortened by the government. Along with the amount you can catch. They act like we're gonna run out of fish. Damn bureaucratic idiots. Anyway. What can we do for y'all?"

"Well. We were hoping to find you and maybe a few others to do some fishing for us. By us, I mean a really big and growing group in Lake Jackson. We're a few hundred strong now. Everyone helping each other. Come to think of it. We are now about thirty more strong. Found some more down on Quintana beach. A couple of them are with us on the bridge to come meet the rest of the group. They've done a great job of clearing out that beach front. Unless a new one wanders onto it, it's good for settling. Just a thought if you're interested."

"I like the idea of eating something besides fish. I would love to trade. We need your help getting off this boat though. Gonna have to kill a hell of a lot of them and we ain't got the arms for it. No guns at all except a flare gun and a small pistol."

"We can do that for you. We brought plenty of ammo. We knew we'd be out a couple days. We'll bring more guns and ammo for you later in case they stop by for dinner again. I know you have more infected in town, I just don't know if they will head this way. I would think the smell of the sea might bring more to you."

"I've got some fish you can take now also. Not a lot but we'll go back out tomorrow. Can you come back in three days? Maybe with some new food? We could sure use it. I can call on the radio when we are coming in if it helps."

"Awesome idea. We can definitely do that. Do you need anything from Wal-Mart or something we may have found along the way?" Aaron pulled out his cell to type himself some notes. Even if they died, they could still be useful for something. Even if they just became paperweights or to throw at zombies.

"More high-end fishing poles and line. Going to go through a lot of it over time. Some fresh clothes would be nice. Can't get home or do laundry. You know?"

"Got it. If you come up with more, text me." Aaron gave him his cell number. "Even if they don't sound right, texts will still go through for a little longer I hope. If it doesn't, radio us. I'll give that to you, too."

"Cool. I know of a couple more out at sea right now. They're staying off shore because of all this. I'll let them know about Quintana. Can you relay to them about the ships; so no one gets shot? Would make life easier if they had somewhere to go."

"No problem there. Tell them to wait till tomorrow though so they can see them approaching. Also, so no one gets shot." Smiling, he shook Casey's and Elliot's hands goodbye. Wayne did the same.

"Look forward to seeing you in a few days. Good to meet you both."

"We'll take care of your current problem. Maybe you can get off the boat for a while if you want. Probably take about thirty minutes. We'll honk when done. Good night, sir."

Making their way back to shore, a particularly pretty zombie came staggering towards them. Wayne made the comment, "Damn, she is fine."

"Sure. Last week. Now she's missing an ear and has a limp."

"Don't be an anti-handy-capable jerk. That's not Politically Correct."

"Oh, shut up, freak. I think you're just ready to climb up on anything with a pulse. She could be fun for about half a minute and then UGH!, you're zombie meat. Or worse. I would have to shoot you." Aaron took half second and shot the poor girl in the chest.

"Damn, she was pretty. Damn jackass, whoever caused this. What a waste. And hell yeah, I'm ready for some lovin'. I'm almost seventeen and still a virgin. Just like you."

"Hold it down, dumbass. Don't need everyone hearing about our problems. Let's move. We got some infected to mow down so we can get on to the hardware store."

"Yes, sir." Wayne playfully punched his brother's arm. A little hard for an explanation point though. He realized it and then he ran. No point in letting Aaron hit him back.

Once they were back to the little caravan of vehicles, they explained the situation. With some hashing out help, the plan was to walk over the bridge and move towards the mobs one at a time. Fully loaded and packed with extra ammo of course. They all took some extra time resupplying and packing each magazine they could find. After that was done, each of them grabbed a bashing weapon of some sort; baseball bat, tire iron, piece of wood left in the back of a truck, an axe, machete, and even one sword. Kylar had taken a cue from Michonne of *The Walking Dead* and come prepared. One good cut and a zombie will fall down and go boom.

Leaving two people behind to watch their backs, those without hand weapons, they walked over the half of the bridge and took a left toward some pretty entranced feverheads. Fish and seagull pieces were flying from munching mouths and flailing arms. To conserve ammunition, only a couple people would take single shots until it became an issue of too many Zs. In the middle of the second group, one teenage infected raised its head and had a raccoon tail hanging from its mouth. After a second of just staring, Jose shot it through its pie-hole. Sucking out the juice from a raccoon tail. Just weird, he thought.

The first couple of groups went down without problems, then the next and another. Two more left along the short stretch of road they were working. That's when it got messy. The sounds from the shooting finally got them to notice something other than food. Threats were somewhere, and they weren't going to stand for it. Well, maybe that was what was going through their minds. Who really knew what was in the mind of an infected animal.

"Form up a line. Danny, watch our backside. This is going to get gruesome." Aaron yelled out.

"As if that raccoon tail guy wasn't gruesome enough? That was fucking gross." Jose fired off a couple double-taps and watched as two munchers fell.

"True dat." Wayne reiterated Jose's feelings.

"Fire off slowly but aim true. If they get within twenty feet, let it rip." Aaron threw a few of his own double-taps into the mix and then changed magazines.

A mass of thirty or more came after them with still more behind continuing to feast. With at least fifty yards between them, the men all just took single or double shots. Still trying to conserve ammo, they were taking them down in very small groups. Only five made it to the twenty-foot mark and met up with a fusillade of bullets. Two made it past that; meeting up with a sword slash through the neck and an axe into the forehead. The first infected's head went bouncing across the pavement and settled at Jose's feet while the second kept staggering into Danny. Mouth still moving but no connection to what was left of its mind. The axe handle moved with it and smacked Danny in the nose. He pushed the zombie away and Wayne put it down with a tire iron to the head. Now it was dead and knew it. Danny was using his shirt to try and stop the flow of blood running down his face.

"Goddamn zombie. My fucking nose. Did he break it?"

Warren took a look at it and pulled out a handkerchief and held it to Danny's nose. "Not broken. Just nailed it pretty good. Put your head back for a few minutes and pinch the bridge. Should stop within five minutes. Might purple up on you but you'll be fine next week." He helped Danny out a second and then said, "It will give you some sympathy with your girl when you get back. You've been in battle and gotten wounded. Might even get you a little extra lovin'." Laughing, he picked his weapon back up and took Danny's while he dealt with his nose.

"Hey, Wayne, let's clean up the rest. Only five left."

"Gotcha. Let me reload real quick." He pulled out another full magazine off the bandolier across his chest.

Aaron hadn't seen it till now. "Where the hell did you get that getup? I just now noticed it."

"Oh, found this in one of the houses on Surfside. You were moving on to the next one already. Forgot to tell you. Whoever lived there had a bunch of stuff but cleared almost all of it out already. You could see where his gun placements were, and he had a couple safes too. I wish I could have seen what was in those if the guns were outside them. But yeah. I got a couple good items. He left some cool knives and how do you think Kylar got the Katana sword? What? He pull it out of his ass?"

"Shut up, dork. I have too much on my mind to care what you are doing or carrying."

"You've been saying shut up a lot lately. What's up with that?"

"Well. It might be because you won't shut up. Moron."

"Butt munch."

"All right. Just shut up and shoot." With that they both opened up and took the rest down. A few minutes later they were back at the trucks and checking on the others. They had only had to kill one infected, so all was good. From there, off they went to Lake Hardware and stocked up for home.

Heading back up Highway 288, Jose called out on the radio for a stop up ahead. Still with about three hours of daylight, Aaron let him. He pulled ahead, and a couple more blocks up he drove into a parking lot. It was a little store but any man in the area knew it well. There were five of them in the surrounding small cities. Peter's Liquor would be a godsend to many. Aaron saw this as a good idea too. A great many needed something to cope nowadays and having a nip every so often could take the edge off.

The parking lot was small though, so Aaron and Warren drove across the street to the Sonic and would load up whatever they could there. A couple slushes would be nice too if they could get it to work. Unfortunately, it looked as if Sonic had been ransacked already so there wasn't much in the way of food for them to take. After about fifteen minutes and with Warren's help, they did get the slushy machine working. Not wanting to give away their surprise, the boys made a crapload of different ones and packed them up in carrying trays. Once done, they went back over to the liquor store.

The others were just about done packing everything they could into the pickups. They left the beds and trailers open for their needed supplies. Jose argued that Jack Daniels was a needed supply, but he was overruled. So, they were only allowed to fill the cabs. Hopefully they could come back later and get even more. Aaron finally got everyone moving again an hour later.

They were all extremely happy with the drinks though. For Kylar, it was his first time having a slush. He was a very health conscience person before the fall. He still wanted to stay in shape, but the times had made that easier what with the constant work needing done. He could afford a splurge day.

Just as Kylar was trying to hop in the truck, two infected males came barreling after him from the road along the parking lot. Just as he turned around, the first one slammed into him. Cherry slush was no part of his wardrobe and causing him to get a little nipply. Those things are cold. Outraged, he flat out punched the first one in the nose, knocking it back a few feet and causing it to stumble to the ground.

The second feverhead was almost to him as he side-stepped and slammed its face into the door frame. A loud crunch could be heard from something in the things face breaking. Not waiting for it to turn back after him, he grabbed it by the head and shoved its face back into the door two more times. Slumping to the ground, possibly dead, Kylar let go. Biter number one was trying to get up so Kylar teed him up like a football. Extra point is good. He kicked it so hard that the zombie's head whipped sideways with a slight crack. It might not have killed it, but no one thought it would be moving anytime. That sound made it seem as if he was now a 'Christopher Reeve'. *'May Superman rest in peace.'*

"Dammit. I was enjoying that. Why did it have to be me?"

"Well, shit. I'm glad it was with the way you just handled those two. Hot damn, son. Where did you learn to fight like that?" Charlie was in awe of this young man.

"Took a couple years of karate and then started training in MMA last year for fun." Looking down at his handiwork, he said, "I guess it was all worth it."

"Damn right it was worth it." Charlie turned to the others. "From now on, he stays with me for any outing. I claim him as my bodyguard." This caused them all to laugh heartily.

"Here, Kylar. We made a few extra. You want cherry again or green apple?" Wayne had brought them both over to Kylar.

"Green Apple. The cherry was good while it lasted, now I want to try something new. New again, anyway." Taking the proffered drink, he sipped in a long one. "Oh, yeah. That's the ticket. I wonder what it would be like to put the two together. Green Apple and Cherry Slush. Damn, that sounds good."

"Let's get the hell out of here. We got a hardware store to hit still."

They arrived back later that night to a very happy mother. Ann nearly squeezed her two boys to death in gratefulness of their being okay. William, Michael, Davis, Steve, and even Sam Howell came up to meet Charlie and the few new people he brought with him. Right beside Sam was Penelope Faucet as usual. She had been inseparable from him since he saved her from her captors a few days back. They had been part of the Corpus group but came up to Lake Jackson to help out. Being that the Corpus contingent had a few doctors already and Penelope needed a change of scenery.

Sam was an excellent doctor and considered an impromptu part of the governing body. Michael felt he should be involved in meeting new people and any of the major decisions that would be discussed. Terry Jackson would normally be here too. He was another Michael thought should be on the 'Knights of the Round Table' group. He being a Navy Seal and the man training the rank and file to fight. Which is what he was currently doing. Finishing up some hand to hand with a dozen future fighters; including William's little girls. Never too early to learn since it was always a constant unknown of when you might have to fight for your life.

Chapter 20

NAS, Corpus Christi

Wednesday, October 30th

A man moved up to the edge of a three-story rooftop holding binoculars. He was camouflaged in an urban style netting while keeping a close eye on what was happening at the Naval Air Station. He didn't need their aircraft watching him watching them. His job was to be covert. For now. Keep watch and report. The man knew there were others across the nation doing the same thing but had no way to know how many or where.

Once firmly in place, he took meticulous notes of how many people he could see, including children. The fencing and gate work near the ocean was new and almost done. The armaments were unknown, but he could note the aircraft that were exposed. Throughout the first day, he saw several vehicles go back and forth. Each unloaded of supplies and then sent out again. These people were busy. He almost admired them for trying to rebuild. Then he remembered that he might have to help bring about their destruction later.

Mid-morning, it looked like some heavy hitters came in for a landing. The Chinook set down gently and out came several people. From what he could see, a few civilians and three heavily armed operators as their escort. A few of the navy regulars saluted the man in front wearing civilian clothes so he took note of this. The man was obviously important; possibly in charge.

A large group was gathered together for a discussion of some sort. About thirty minutes later, they broke up with most going back inside. A few minutes after, three pairs of Humvees and large trucks left in different directions.

After a few more hours, the vehicles all trickled back. Watching through his binoculars, he saw each of the big trucks was full of clothing, boxes, and bags of something. Adjusting his glasses, he marveled. Costumes and candy. *'Party?'* Children were going back and forth, carrying costumes along the way. Presumably to try them on or something. Well. He just kept writing about it all. Not having any real idea what he was going to end up doing, he wanted as much information as he could find.

After a little while later, the loaded trucks all moved towards the gates and stopped. Some of the older children jumped up and into them. A few Humvees, pickups, and cars all pulled up and children of all ages loaded into them too; carrying their costumes and bags or whatever with them. It looked as if just about every person under eighteen, and several adults, were leaving. Interesting.

The gates rolled back after all the vehicles were packed to the gills. He heard before he saw more trucks coming down the road. Just before the others left the base, a rolling convoy of school buses, Humvees, more pickups, and Deuce and a half trucks went driving by. Honking and waving out the windows, they kept moving and the base's own convoy fell in behind them. Very interesting indeed. He had no way of knowing where they were going and there wasn't time for him to get downstairs to follow. So, he stayed in place and made a call.

"Go for control."

"Beach Bum here. Got an informative situation."

"Hold one." Control went through some files till she found the one marked Beach Bum. Then responded again. "Okay. Go."

"A couple dozen vehicles of various sorts just rolled out somewhere. Most came from another location and then the air station rolled theirs right along with them. Most of the occupants were children, maybe a hundred or more. Can't follow in time to find out where."

"Hold your station. Keep your observations going. I'll run this up the flagpole and get back with you. Anything else?"

"No, ma'am. Just figured y'all ought to know. Nothing else out of the ordinary here. They're just fortifying the perimeters, including the waterways, from the infected."

"Good. Out." With that, control hung up. Looking at the phone for a second, he put the antenna down and put it away. He backed away from the ledge and walked around the roof door area to the back of it. Whipping out his Johnson, he let loose a long stream while he contemplated what he saw. By the time he was done, the only thing he came up with was they were taking all of the kids to a better location. And maybe they were going to have a costume party? *'Oh well'*, he thought. *'Whatever'*. He laid back down under his cover and took a nap.

"Major Bharata, sir. You have a call from Fort Hood. General Willoughby wants a word." The ensign had run over to where Bert was having breakfast. Two buildings over from the radio nest.

"Thank you. On my way." He ate another bite of eggs, took a sip of orange juice, and grabbed his coffee to go. The ensign waited for him, even though he hadn't needed to. They went together at a fast walk.

"General Willoughby, sir. This is Major Bertram Bharata. How can I help you?"

"I hear you're the man in charge and doing a damn good job so far."

"Thank you, sir. I got thrust into this position and I have a great many good men and women behind me."

"Hard to keep everyone safe today, I know that. Whatever you need, if I can provide, I will. On to my call. I have heard through the grapevine that is rampant radio city now, that you have a Senator Fred Cruz running around."

"Yes, sir. Amazed you know already. I guess the rumor mill is full. I won't say over the radio where he is, but, yes. Safe and in a hell of a compound with others of like-mindedness."

"If it's possible, can you arrange for him to come here and meet with me? I would like to chat with him about our future. And my people plan on putting up a hell of a shindig for Halloween. They need it and I wholeheartedly concur. We were lucky enough to be able to house and shelter a very large number of families. Even civilians from Killeen. I have roving guards around the entire population perimeter. Place is too big to get it all, but I can protect the people at least."

"Sounds like you have a sound arrangement. What about food?"

"Several families already had good gardens going but it obviously isn't enough. We have some greenhouses already set up to help from bad weather along with a great many people planting and seeding a nice portion of land. On top of that, we have been raiding grocery stores, big box stores, and any food places near here. Sending out more people further each day. We should be good for our future. Funny how the apocalypse brings so many different people together to help each other."

"True. Seems like all that racial BS just disappears. No left or right politics to bog down a person's life. Any issues with command or anything like that, sir?"

"No. Everyone knows I'm in charge here. Just like before. I have changed my way of leading of course. No one giving me commands anymore so I have gathered all my Majors and Colonels as a sort of my own Joint Chiefs. I realize that I will not always be right."

"Same here, sir. They put me in charge, but I have a Warrant Petty Officer of my Seal Team that is my military strategist and a circle of good men and women to help me with bigger decisions." Bert took a sip of coffee and started in again. "Well, sir. I will give the senator a call right now and give him your channel info. Do you have a cell he can call also? Might be easier if it stays up and working well enough."

"Sure. It is (202) 555-5309. Still based out of Washington, D.C. I guess it's easier for the higher ups. At least, I guess it was."

"All right. I'm on it. Talk soon and let me know if there's anything I can do. Out."

"Good day, son. Over and out."

Using a cell because it is still easier than talking on a radio, he called John Parks. "Hey, John, this is Bert. Got a couple minutes?"

"Sure. We're just working on more of the warehouse wiring and stuff. Still trying to make everything more livable so we can accommodate anyone else that comes along."

"Always thinking, I see. I have a request of the senator and yourself if you are up for it. General Stephen Willoughby from Fort Hood has asked for a meet and greet with Mr. Cruz. And he wants y'all to be there for their Halloween party tomorrow night. Think you can do it?"

"I don't see why not. As long as Fred wants to, that is. I can talk to him. Maybe we can do it first thing in the morning. Text me his info. If I don't get it in the next two hours, I will radio you. Never know how the cell service is going to act."

"Good deal. Will do. You're right about the phones. We're starting to get some good static interference down here. Now get back to work."

"You have a good day, too."

John hung up and walked over to the senator. Fred was receptive to meeting those at Fort Hood and thought it was a good idea to wait till the next morning. Once word got around, his wife, Sheila, and John's girlfriend all wanted to go with them. Along with Jack, Peter, and a couple other former military operators. During the evening dinner, they would hash out the fly-in and operational security measures for the morning.

Chapter 21

U.S.S. Lexington, Corpus Christi

Aboard the aircraft carrier museum, children were running around everywhere. Most of the kids had gone on to the Timmons's farm but there were way too many for just one run. So, the rest just kept being kids; having fun doing whatever. Some of the volunteers left over from pre-Zombieville were watching over them and making sure none went overboard. They knew the kids needed to exercise but safety must still be maintained. Children, younger and older, were also helping plant seeds for later. Since the aircraft currently occupying the carrier would never fly again, they were using cockpits, turbines, and any other crevice they could to put in vegetables that would grow in direct sunlight. Many others were being potted however they could on the next deck below where you first walk onto the museum piece.

Most of their food was being brought in from area restaurants and grocery stores but they still had much in the cafeterias also. The children were also being taught how to fish near the shoreline but were always overseen by armed security when on the docks or beach. Too many infected still milling about the Corpus Christi area. It would take a lot of work to drive them all back or kill them.

Some of the older teenagers and parents would go out with military men to scavenge. There was plenty of food out there still, but it takes time to get it and bring it back each day. They utilized whatever help they could get on the Lexington. This day was no different.

Two vehicles, a Humvee and a pickup with a trailer, rolled out towards the eastern most edge of Corpus. This was the furthest out they had been this way if you didn't count Bert's trip to Lake Jackson. The plan was to try and hit the Northshore Country Club in Portland. This was across the water from Corpus and a former member said there would be a great amount of food, water, and beverages awaiting them. Prime pickings.

Consisting of four navy personnel, two parental men, and three sixteen and seventeen-year olds, the caravan almost made it to the club. Almost. Rounding the final corner to the entrance they were bracketed by sudden and ferocious gunfire. It lit up the Humvee and starred the windshield. The driver slammed the truck into reverse and slammed right into the truck behind it. Turning to those in his vehicle, he yelled for everyone to get out and head back to the truck. His front passenger didn't move. Some of the gunfire had made it through the windshield and peppered the poor man all about his upper torso. He was gone.

Cursing, he opened his door and started firing back. Ensign Jacque LeBeaux laid down suppressing fire while his crew got out and ran. Gunfire kept coming, shooting into the vehicle like the passengers were still in there. Once he saw the others away, he moved backwards, firing as he shuffled. Getting to the back of the other truck, he checked and made sure everyone else made it but his copilot.

"We can't stay here. We need to get to that building. I think that's the clubhouse. Everyone got that?!"

A round of nods and some very horrified expressions came back to him. "Stay near the tree line until we are right beside it. Regroup there. Go!" He laid down more fire as the others all took off, crouching and running. One of the parents took a round across the bicep and stumbled. The seventeen-year-old picked him up and they got moving again. Running and firing with a fresh magazine, LeBeaux moved last. Just as he got to the safety of the trees, he took a round through the fleshy part of his left calf. Limping and rushing, he kept going. Before all of this came down on them, he had planned to try out for the Seal Teams but that crashed to a halt when the virus reared its ugly head. With that type of mental toughness though, there was no way he was going to not get these people to safety. Help those that can't help themselves. That was his job.

All of them made it through the trees and were within twenty feet of the side of the building. The fire was still chewing up the wooded area but no longer were any bullets winging their way. Instead of trying for the front door, LeBeaux directed them to the back door. They would be out of the line of sight from any stray bullets and a little safer. Reaching the back door first, the teenagers had to shoulder the door open the hard way. It had been locked, but with determination, that was just a small obstacle to overcome. LeBeaux was the last in, limping on his injured leg but not in any real danger. The fire started to taper off as they re-secured the door as well as they could.

Peering through the windows here and there, they could see several men working their way through the trees. Search and destroy was their mission. Being one of three military members left, he tried to post them all up at strategic locations along the side towards the enemy. Making sure the civilians knew to keep their heads down, he went looking for some alcohol and first aid supplies. He knew there had to be some somewhere inside because this was the welcome lodge for the country club. Today's businesses always kept small kits around. Someone might stub their little toe on a parking bump. That kind of thing actually happened a lot with woman in open toe shoes and men running around in sandals. For some reason, people just couldn't pick up their feet when in those types of shoes. Even LeBeaux had done it before.

He found a bottle of scotch in the bottom of one of the administrator's cabinets and took a big swig of it. Then he poured it onto his wound to do a cursory cleaning. Gritting his teeth, he made only a small whimper. Then he moved into the break room and searched through all the cabinets and drawers there. Bingo. He found a medium size box with everything to tend his bullet crease. Band-aids, gauze, Neosporin, scissors, and other items of need. It even included a small sewing kit.

Bringing the bottle and kit out to where the others were, he handed the scotch to the other injured party. He told the man to pour some on his wound, but to take the pain as quietly as possible. After a big swig and a grimace, he did as he was told. He let out a slightly louder sound of pain than

LeBeaux did. On instinct, Jacque looked through the windows for any sign the bad guys might have heard it. Nothing. Whew was all the ensign could think. Taking care of the man first, he got ready to bandage his arm before he took care of his own wound. Pouring more onto the area of the flesh wound, the man made another small sound and then Jacque put on some Neosporin and a bandage to help start the healing process.

Afterward, he was next. Taking another much bigger drink, he tensed and poured some on his own much worse wound. The bullet had been a through and through, but it was bleeding pretty good. He was going to have to stitch it up. Before he could though, one of the men at the windows yelled, "Get down!" Heavy fire started ripping through the windows in the main area where they were all gathered. One of them had been spotted while looking out and started their own little war.

"Jacque. Looks like seven vatos. Do-rags and all, man. I think they had the same idea as us." One of the other ensigns, a young woman by the name of Patricia Talbot, told him.

"All right. Fire a couple shots here and there but conserve your ammo. The rest of us; we're going to spread out across the rest of the side and try and take them down from separate windows. Any questions?" None came except one.

"Should a couple of us post up on the doors just in case?" The second parent was thinking smartly.

"Good idea. How about the two parents do that while the rest of us take different firing points. I'll tell you when to fire. Just find a target and wait. If we do this all at the same time, we might surprise them. Or at least catch them in a crossfire. Let's move."

Each moved along the building. A clear line of sight was all through this side, from front door to rear. The parents each stood on the side of their respective doors, behind where they would open. As Jacque watched and waited, he lined up one particularly sneaky raghead. He was wearing a greasy, stained, white wife-beater tank top and even dirtier tan cargo pants. Sneakers of the top of the line variety Nikes, a Fu Manchu type mustache, and a Mexican flag do-rag on his head. This dirtbag was rocking the whole gangbanger getup to the hilt. Like an extra from a really bad eighties drug movie.

"I've got the small tank top with the mustache. Call out your targets. Try not to double up unless you need to."

Each of the window watchers did as told. This would leave one left if they were able to take them all down. That was a big if since he didn't know if the kids could shoot. When each had called one, he gave the go ahead. Six shots rolled through the building and then a few more as some came peppering back at them. Fu Manchu went down like a sack of potatoes as a round went punching through the bridge of his nose and out the back of his head. The Mexican flag flew for about three seconds before it landed on his chest like a badge of honor. Ha. Honor. Like any of these pieces of shit know what that is.

One of his personnel took one through the chest and he was gone within just a few seconds. Cursing, LeBeaux sighted in on anything else he could find. The seventeen-year-old had punched his man right through the chest and was already sighting in on another target. One of the younger teenagers had missed and then had to dive from the fusillade coming back at him. One shot rang out from the older kid and another sack of trash went down. He and Jacque both sighted on the same man after that. One that had taken a shoulder shot and was firing into Patricia's window, keeping her pinned down. Two shots flew, two shots hit, and parts of the man's head went flying. One slightly higher than the other had penetrated through his neck and mouth. Nearly taking the whole head off. Jacque looked down at the older teenager and gave him a nod of respect.

"Button it up, guys. There's still one out there. There could be more and we haven't seen them yet. Double up on the doors in case. The rest of you keep a close eye out the windows. I'm going to the other side of the building. He might be trying to sneak up on us." Everyone did as told. Even though the other military members were all of the same rank, they took his orders and obeyed. People flock to natural leaders. Especially since their Petty Officer had been the one in the passenger seat.

Still bleeding but fired up with adrenaline, LeBeaux moved off to the other side. Moving from room to room, he noticed a window was open in the restroom. Carefully, he did a spatial check of the prior room before moving into the bathroom. It was a small room, and no one was in it, but he knew that meant nothing. If someone had come through, he could already be moving through the back of the building and coming up on the rest of the group without them knowing it.

Still moving slowly, he stalked through each of the offices until he saw a shadow up ahead. Almost upon the back door where he knew an adult and teenager would be posted up. No way in hell would he lose another to these shits. Moving faster and with purpose, he came up near the man just as he was raising his weapon. Jacque put one round into the guys back and then hit him over the head for good measure. The man managed to get off one shot, but it was into the floor as he was going to the ground. The man was alive but almost unconscious. Grabbing him by the collar, LeBeaux began to interrogate him before he died.

"How many of you are there?"

"Fuck off." He spit up some blood as he said this.

"Tell me or I'll let you die. I can help you but only if you answer my questions."

"Fine. Fine. Eight."

"There are eight of you?"

"Yeah. Here. Many more at our compound. They gonna kill you, punta."

"But only eight of you came here?"

"Yeah. Now, help me."

"Are you telling me the truth? Everything?"

"Yeah, motherfucker. Now help me. I can't feel my legs."

"Damn. That has to suck."

"You promised. Help me."

"I lied. I don't negotiate with terrorists. And that's what you are. A domestic terrorist."

"You bastard." He tried to pull a knife from his pocket and Patricia put a bullet in his head.

"Yeah. That's what you get, dipshit. Thanks, Pat." LeBeaux stood and immediately fell down. The blood loss was getting to him. The others helped him back into the main room when one of the ensigns that had still been watching out yelled.

"Got a runner. Too far and obscured for me to tag. Want me to chase?"

Weakly, Jacque said, "No. Let him go. We have to grab whatever we can carry now and get out of here. Braindead back there said there were more at a compound. We're gonna have company if we don't move."

"Pat, come with me. Let's get the trucks." Pat moved out with the ensign. While they were gone, they patched up Jacque's leg with more scotch, some quick and makeshift sewing, and a rather large amount of bandage material. He would need help getting into the Humvee but definitely live. The trucks pulled up to the front of the building and they threw in as many supplies as they could find within a few minutes. The second vehicle had a lot of front end damage, but they would take it as far as it would drive. Once they could get LeBeaux into the hummer, they were tearing out of there at speed. Several zombies were making their way across the course, brought out by all the gunfire. As they would around the front gate and gone, a great many more could be seen.

"I hope that sum'bich got eaten before he could get back to his banger friends." Pat said this aloud to no one in particular.

"Oh, if we could get that lucky." Jacque commented just before he passed out. It was a pretty uneventful trip back and they were all grateful. Especially since the second truck made it through the gates of the air station just as the radiator started to spew steam. God was still mostly on their side. Too bad they had to lose two of their own in the process.

Chapter 22

Corpus Christi Medical Center, Midday

"Shit, Vinny. This is going to be a clusterfuck." Jim Lee was scanning the front of the hospital.

The whole area, entrance to a full parking lot, had zombies everywhere just...roaming. The doors to the hospital were either wide open or shattered, they couldn't see them clearly enough. Scattered bodies, decaying or barely there, were lying all over. Some partially in cars and around the front doors or in the street. Hell had come down on this cluster of buildings and had not been kind in its taking of lives.

"Yeah. We're going in the back. Trying to take the front would be time consuming. Not to mention ammo heavy. Let's see where Bert said they escaped from. Maybe it will be easier."

Still a couple blocks away from the hospital, they took the long way around. The back gates were wide open but only a few of the infected milled about. Including the zombie strippers that

Bert had mentioned. Still pretty but definitely the worse for wear. Wild hair and as grimy as a girl could get after a week and a half without a bath or hygiene.

"What a waste, man. I wonder if we throw a couple twenties at them if they would still give us a lap dance. You know. Muscle memory." Papa cracked himself up.

"What the hell is wrong with you? Dork." Not seeing much opposition, Vinny kept driving. Watching the two 'ladies' while he drove. They started moving their way. Slowly though. As if they were still traumatized from losing their two friends a week ago. They made it to the back-warehouse doors without attracting any other attention so far. Getting out of the Humvee armed and ready, the two girls stopped heading their direction. Then turned and ran away.

"Yep. Guess they still don't wanna die. Interesting though how some of them act." Jim Lee kept watch on the corner of the building.

Vinny and Papa walked up to the back door. Partially open, Vinny peered in through the crack. "I see two, but I think I can hear a few more. You ready for some 'Hop N Pop'?"

"On you."

With Jim watching their backs, Vinny held up three fingers and counted down. On one, they burst through the doors, left and right tracking. Each of their weapons let off a couple suppressed 'pfft's and moved on. First two down. As they crept through, one more to the left turned their way and Papa put it down.

Just as they were almost done clearing the room, a heavy-set older man came down on Vinny from the short side of a holding rack. Vinny didn't have the time to sweep his rifle up and went down under the man's bulk. Using the rifle to keep teeth off of him by shoving it into the man's mouth, he pushed him over so he was back on top. Popping fatboy's nose a couple times with a gloved right fist, he was able to leverage the rifle into his throat while he pulled out his knife. Just before he lost his advantage, Vinny slid the knife into the man's right temple and quieted him for good. He got up and wiped the knife on the infected's shirt and re-sheathed it.

"Did you get a good workout in there, boss?" Smiling, Papa was glad Vinny was okay, but you had to rib each other.

"Yeah, actually. Good pump going. Now shut up and go get Jim Lee." Vinny, also smiling, did a quick double check of the warehouse area and then went up to the double doors leading into the rest of the hospital.

"Hey, Jim. All clear inside."

"That's good because we're fixing to have company. Those dancers brought back friends. Get inside now! We have to barricade till we're ready to leave."

As soon as they were inside, they started throwing big items in front of the doors and locked them. Jim Lee hung something over the small window too. No sense in letting them see inside and watch their prey. Once done, they watched both ends for a minute. Hearing movement outside, they got ready for any incursion. Nothing. Not one of them tried to get inside or even worked the door. Yep. Braindead. Good. Feeling safe enough, they moved up to the inside doors and watched inside.

"I don't see anything, yet. Let's try to conserve ammo and kill quietly. Jim, you stay on fire duty. Papa and I will use knives. Don't let me get killed though. That would make me very unhappy."

"On it, boss."

With that, Vinny and Papa pulled out their blades. Two fisting them, they crept through the doors and into the building. Being the bottom floor, they expected the most resistance. Unless an infected person made it up before they turned, the odds of very many being on the upper floors were pretty slim. Seeing two bigger infected males leaning over something in the middle of the hallway, they kept creeping. As they got closer, it looked as if they were eating on a smaller woman. Coming up quietly, they each grabbed a handful of hair and put their knives through a skull. Once done, looking down upon their meal, they could see that the person was still fresh and had scratches all over their arms.

"Are they eating their own?" Papa quietly whispered.

"Maybe. Would be logical if they have no other source of food. Keep going."

Clearing this wing didn't take much more. Only three others were easily dispatched. The doors to the next area were closed and putting an ear to them, shuffling and groaning could easily be heard on the other side. Not wanting to go there yet, they found a broom and some ties. Using them on the doors, they secured the room as capably as possible. That was one entrance they wouldn't have to worry about until they were ready. Having completely canvassed this lower floor wing, they stalked toward the stairs. No reason to take the elevators. There's no telling what's on them and no one wanted to get stuck in one if the power suddenly, finally went out.

Popping open the door as quietly as possible, Jim surveyed the upper staircase while Vinny moved down to the basement doors. Using some more zip ties, he secured them too till they could get back to them later. Coming back up, he silently directed Jim Lee to take point. It would be harder for them to fight hand to hand in the staircase than to just pop an infected in the chest if needed.

They made it to the second floor and slowly opened the door to the inside of the hospital. Immediately in front of them was a white lab coated individual. It looked as if they were writing something in front of them, leaning on the counter top. Not seeing anyone else, Vinny spoke quietly.

"Doctor. Are you okay? Is there..." That was all he got out before the 'doctor' turned and attacked.

The front of his coat was soaked in dried and some still wet blood, viscera, and other unknowns. Deep scratches were welting up across his cheek, but it wasn't phasing him at the moment. He screeched and ran at Vinny. Hands in claw-like gestures to rip and shred. Still with his blades at the ready, Vinny swept the man to the side and his head bounced off of the near wall.

Putting all of his weight into the man's back, Vinny drove one of his knives into the base of the skull and let him fall to the floor.

That was just the beginning, unfortunately. The doctor's screeching brought out a multitude of infected. More doctors, nurses, and patients came screaming down the halls from all sides. The second floor was gone. Whatever medicines here would have to wait till they could sweep it clear. Just like the rest of the bottom floor. It would take a heavy fire group to just wade in at another time.

They backpedaled through the stair door and put their backs to it to stop the feverheads from crashing through. Opening toward the staircase, they had to hold the door closed while Jim Lee tried to secure it. Double and triple wrapping the handle down, they were finally able to back off of the door. They watched it shake from the pounding on the other side for a few minutes to ensure it stayed closed. Some of the vitriol from the infected subsided and slacked off quite a bit after five minutes. Short attention spans. Another case of a dog with a 'Squirrel!' complex.

Blowing off some of their excitement in big puffs of air, they moved up the stairs. Third floor was next. Prepared a little more, Vinny opened the door. Or tried to. It was secured from the other side. Not locked but maybe tied off. He tried to wrench it open, but it wouldn't budge. Maybe there was life inside. Taking a chance, he spoke softly.

"Hello. Anyone in there?" He listened but didn't hear anything. "Hello. Is there someone inside?" This time he heard a noise. Not sure what it was, he waited a few more seconds and then called again. "Hello. My name is Vinny. Anyone in there?"

"Yes. Yes. We're alive. Who are you?"

"I'm Warrant Officer Vincent Dupree, ma'am. Navy Seal. Are you okay in there?"

"There are seven of us. We are hungry but alive. No one up here is bitten or scratched. I am going to undo some of the chains. Can you show me some ID?"

"The only thing I have is my Seal patch and my word, ma'am. A fellow doctor sent us. Major Bertram Bharata. We came here looking for meds and survivors. Looks like I scored on one of them so far." He slid his patch through the sliver of space the lady had allowed. Each of them showed their faces to her. She passed the patch back through.

"Bert's alive? Really? Give me a second. I have to talk to the others."

"No problem, ma'am. We can wait." After a couple minutes of deliberation, she came back and undid the rest of the bindings on the door. Once open, Vinny held his hands up, so she could see that all of his armaments were put away and not currently a threat. Papa did the same. Jim Lee still had his rifle out and at the ready though. As soon as they were through the doorway and it was reclosed, he dropped it and showed himself to be currently harmless. Kind of. Were any of them truly harmless, even unarmed? Some of the survivors visibly relaxed at this though. Only two of them still stood in fear.

"Hello. It's so good to see someone. We hardly have any food left and no weapons. Being stuck up here is driving us stir crazy."

"Understandable. I'm Vinny, this is Papa and Jim Lee. We are all Seals. The Naval Air Station is under our control and completely safe. Bert is the highest rank there. A natural leader. We have a lot of people and even children. Some of them are at the Lexington and a ranch outside of town. You're going to be fine now. We just have to get you out of here."

"Wow. Bert made it. Thank God. And thank you."

After introductions went around, Vinny found out that they now had two more doctors, a few nurses and a couple patients and family. None so bad they couldn't walk though. That was a great plus. Vinny told her to relock the door behind them though. They still had one more floor to check out. Doctor Sarah Sungh, the lady that seemed to be in charge, informed him that they had heard noises upstairs but had no way of knowing who or what was up there. Just before he went back out the door, he asked that they start rounding up as many medicines and items they could take. She nodded an affirmative and got the others started on that task. Thanking her, they got ready and left again.

When they got to the top floor landing, there was a body next to the door. Still alive but in such bad shape, the teenage girl didn't move much. It tried to lunge at them but just fell flat on her face. Vinny stepped up and put the blade through the top of her blond head. A mercy killing. It looked as if she was so hungry and emaciated in just the last week that she could barely move. Pushing her dead form to the side, they opened the door.

No sounds or movement could be seen or heard. They crept through the area slowly. Papa and Vinny on knife patrol again while Jim Lee watched over them with silenced rifle at the ready. They were halfway through searching the floor when they clearly heard movement from a few doors down and to the left.

Leaving Jim Lee there, they made sure to clear the rest of the floor first. Coming back, they slid the door open and peeked inside. It was a normal midsize room with a corpse lying on the bed. An older woman hooked up to a multitude of tubes and wires. All of the machinery was turned off and silent.

Still in stealth mode, they cleared the room easily except for the bathroom. Taking point as he usually did when the whole team wasn't together, Vinny put his hand on the handle and slowly turned it. Yanking it open with his knife at the ready, he scared the literal shit out of a male nurse sitting in the shower stall holding a scalpel. The poor man let out a shriek and defecated himself in fear.

"Sir. It's okay. We're here to help. You can come out." It took the man almost a minute to realize he wasn't about to be eaten and slowly got up. The stench from his bowels was already permeating the air. Papa found another pair of scrubs and handed them to him.

"Why don't you get cleaned up, sir? Come out when you're ready. The area is secure. We'll wait." Papa made no jokes or any of his usual quips in this situation. He sympathized with the poor guy. Living here for over a week, all alone and scared to death. Almost literally. They waited about ten minutes while he took a shower and got dressed. When he came out, he felt refreshed and ready to face the world again. Well, partially. It was a messed-up world he had to face.

"I'm sorry, guys. I just... I thought..." He couldn't quite finish his sentences.

"It's okay. I'm Papa, this is Vinny and Jim Lee. We're Navy Seals. There are more on the floor below alive, too. We're going to get y'all out of here."

"Oh, thank you. I'm Pablo. I was a nurse up here in the cancer ward. I didn't have very many, but I lost the two that stayed. I don't have the expertise to keep them alive and no one else was here to help. Everyone left or was killed in the lower floors. The two that were up here were on their last legs of life and gave it up. I've just been waiting. Either to die or be rescued. Thank you."

"It's all good now, Pablo. We could use your help while we're here. Gather all the medicine and any supplies we can use. Everything we can carry. The local Naval air station is up and running with plenty of other people. You'll be safe but we're going to need medical supplies as we go on."

"On it. There's some trash bags in that storage closet. Grab them and I'll start rounding stuff up." Once Pablo had a task he could sink his teeth into, he was a driven man. He went room by room and threw stuff in each bag as they brought it. The last was the big storage room for the meds. Opening it with his key, he went to town just shoving stuff off of the shelves and into bags. No need to be nice about it. Better to be quick and sort through when in a safer haven.

An hour after leaving the third floor, they were able to return back to the door. A dozen big trash bags were set down near the first-floor door and ready to go to truck. Once he re-established contact on the third, they opened the door and people started bringing their bags too. They had even more useful items awaiting use. Everyone and everything waited downstairs now.

The basement was all that awaited them. Before they moved on, one of the nurses begged them not to go down. She said it had been overrun the first day. That was where she had been when the hospital fell. With this new information, they left it secured and decided it was time to go 'home'. They all grabbed some bags except for Jim Lee. He would be their armed escort, just in case. Everything was brought all the way to the outside door and set aside.

They had one huge problem though. Only one Humvee to carry twelve people. Wasn't going to happen. Especially with all of their newfound booty. Lifting the makeshift window cover, Vinny looked outside. About ten or so infected were still meandering about, looking for them. Explaining the situation to the others, he tried to establish some sort of plan. They needed another vehicle or two. Time to go fishing.

With each of his operators ready to deal death, they removed their cobbled together barricade. Swinging open the door, they started shooting down targets. The semi-quiet 'pfft's rang out over and over. Five, six, eight, then ten were down. All within one minute of leaving the building. Training kicked in and no rounds were wasted. The only infected still standing were the same two 'exotic dancers'. Watching them. Staring back at them, Vinny wondered what the hell was going on inside their minds. A question that would never be answered.

Looking around quickly for a couple bigger vehicles, Jim Lee spotted a UPS truck. As a group, they watched in three directions as they walked over to it. The door was wide open in the front, but the back was still closed. Standing near the front was Jim. Vinny opened the back doors while Papa trained his gun towards them. Empty. Well, that was a small blessing.

The truck was still half full of packages and shelving. Papa jumped inside and stared to remove the shelving while stacking the packages on one side. He planned on keeping the packages too since they had no idea what was inside them. Some of it might be useful. Once enough room was made, he let the others know. Jim Lee jumped in and started the truck up. Keys in the ignitions still and everything. Take the miracles where you could.

They backed it right up to the doors and got everyone loaded. The two dancers were still watching them. Creepy. And mesmerizing considering they were still topless. Getting everyone on board and all of the supplies loaded, Jim Lee volunteered to drive the truck. With everyone else ready, Vinny and Papa walked back to their Humvee. That was when one of the two zombies decided to shriek and ran right at them. A little taken aback, they still both drew their sidearms and shot her in the chest. Two shots; two holes near the heart. She stopped suddenly, looked down, and fell. Dead. Her friend just stood in the same spot and looked at her. Still standing. Still staring. Extremely creepy.

The UPS truck moved out first since it was closest to the exit. Papa drove the Humvee. Both vehicles had to pass right by the body and the live zombie on the way out. The truck got out and turned right at the exit. As the Humvee neared and passed the body, the second stripper stepped over and in front of the Humvee. With no time to react, even if he had wanted to avoid her, he couldn't. The grill smashed into her upper torso and face, grinding it down and then the back-driver's tire thumped over part of her body. Looking back through the mirrors, they could see her twitch. Shaking his head in wonder, Papa pulled out to the right and hit the gas pedal

"Weird, huh?"

"I have no words." Vinny was still looking back at the bodies until they were out of view. "Kick this thing. Let's get in front in case we run into trouble." They did exactly that but had a smooth ride all the way back to the base.

"Truly a weird fucking day."

Chapter 23

A Lazy Lake Jackson Morning, 6am

Already, several dozen men, women, and children were out running the perimeter of the fence lines. All three blocks worth. Calisthenics. That was what Terry was drilling into as many as possible. Or as Germ liked to say; the number one rule *of Zombieland*. Cardio. The indirect quote he told everyone is 'to escape a pursuing zombie, you will need to outrun it." So, jogging was the way Terry had them start the day. His training group had grown over the last couple days. More and more joined, wanting to learn a better way to survive. Most only had the mornings, having other jobs and positions to fill the rest of the day.

They would run for an hour or as far as they could. Most could only walk at first but each day, it would get easier. That's how exercise worked. Terry wasn't going to push any of them too far. He knew he was working with civilians and most were in no shape yet but maybe peared. Or cantaloupe. Hell, he even had a couple watermelons. But he was proud of those that were trying to change. They might live longer.

The hardest thing for them to train on right now was shooting. Any gunfire just brought out more infected and they didn't need that. Not on the grand scale that it might occur. Terry and Germ used their best judgment and trained with any swords, axes, knives, and bats at first. Teaching people how to maneuver and twist for the maximum impact with the minimum effort. This would also help them not expend as much energy when the time came to put down any feverheads. Conserve and reuse whatever fuel you had in your particular tank. Everyone was different. Terry was a very patient man and learned a long time ago that people learned at different speeds. When needed, he would personally demonstrate the best way to do something. Nine times out of ten, the trainee picked it up quicker and excelled.

This morning, after the run/walk, he had everyone line up in the middle of the street. There was a lot of huffing and puffing, so Terry gave them all a couple of much needed minutes. Then he said, 'Ten-hut!' Almost all stood straight up. Even most of the children. Some of the older people had more problems recovering, so he looked them over for another minute.

"I'm proud of you all. It's only been a couple days, but we have had great participation. Some of this stuff you're learning may never even be used but at least you'll be ready. This morning, I want to go over some hand to hand knife use. I had some volunteers make us several fakes. We can only do six groups of two so everyone else will have to sit and watch. We'll rotate you all after ten minutes of training and continue on for the next couple days. Turnball and I will each take three to maximize the learning. Any questions?" There were none and everyone had recovered from the run by this time.

"Good. Let's get to it. We're burning daylight." And they trained. Most had to move on with other chores over the next hour, so they were the first to work with the wooden knives and be back tomorrow. This was how Terry and Germ would spend their time. Neither had any problems with it for they knew that many would live longer because of what they were doing. It was a satisfying lot in the life they had been handed.

Danny, Aaron, Wayne, and several others got ready for an adventurous excursion into the plants. The Freeport area had one of the largest group of chemical blocks in the world. Dow, Olin, and BASF all had business amongst the three areas; Plant A & B to go with Oyster Creek. Not knowing what they may be getting into, they would park a little away from the first plant. One person per truck would stay behind to drive while all the others would walk in. They would have to find some LEL (Lower Explosive Limit) meter. This way they could detect if there was any danger while they moved around. There were too many ways to die in plants, especially when only certain ones were able to shut down in time. Chlorine, propylene, and a myriad of other –enes and –ides could kill.

Stopping at the first row of office trailers, they rummaged through until they found some chemical suits and LEL meters. Being operators before the infected took over, Jose and Kylar walked up the street first to check levels. Staying back, Aaron, Danny, and Wayne walked and watched over them in case any infected attacked. A quarter mile inside the gates, they came upon the first block. No danger yet so they signaled back for the trucks to come forward. This would be a good staging area for everyone and they could start grabbing any water bottles and books available.

While the majority of the guys did that, the operators and the boys both kept going. Commandeering the first block's Kubotas, they were off. They grabbed more suits and air bottles and threw them into the back of each four-wheeler.

There were two more blocks to check out before they got to the one they used to work at. No infected or anyone was seen throughout the whole time. As they approached their block, a stench flowed their way. Along with a growing sound of something indeterminate. They slowed up at the northwest corner and stopped to gather their bearings. Luckily, the blocks all along this part of Plant B were shut down and not emitting any gas of any kind.

"What the hell is that sound?" Jose curiously spoke first.

"Kind of like a moaning with a little crunching and munching added." Danny had a worried look.

"Let's take it slow from here. Slower anyway. Kylar, you and Jose go first again. I hope you wore your hiking boots." Aaron settled into the driver's seat and waited.

"These damn slave drivers. C'mon Jose." They moved down the street to the far corner and stopped again. The sound was much louder and smell much worse. Rounding down southward, they ended their trip at the control room and staff building. Still no explosive levels, they were all out and trying to determine where the sound was coming from. Peering into the distance, Wayne saw something on a far hill.

"What is that? I think I see movement."

"That's the trash mound. Where all of Plant B's garbage goes. Oh. Holy shit! That's it. The sound. Look!" Kylar was pointing up near the top.

"Damn! How many can you see?" Aaron was standing there with his mouth wide open.

"Not many up top but I don't wanna know how many are inside the hill. I bet that's where all those things were heading the other day. Some sort of instinct or... God. I hope they're not communicating somehow. We'd be screwed if they can do that."

"Well shit, Danny. The hill might bring even more while we're here. This could be a bigger problem that it looks like."

"How do you wanna handle this, Aaron? I think we can get everything without gathering their attention."

"Yeah. Let's do it. Radio the trucks and tell them to come up on this side of the block. That way we don't garner extra attention. Let's grab everything we can and get it ready for a quick extraction."

"On it, boss."

They had been able to clear out five blocks of all the water, books, and all other supplies they could find. Exploring a little, Jose and Kylar found that the newest and biggest chlorine block had not been shut down all the way. It was very dangerous to go anywhere near it as there was a rather large cloud blanketing the block. It might stick around for another week as far as they knew. It was unknown where or how big the leak was. But an idea was forming in Danny's head.

"Can we use the chlorine cloud? Maybe drag a bunch of the infected into it. Easy way to kill them off. Won't waste any bullets or anything."

"I like it. Really dangerous though. That means someone has to be bait. While wearing a chemical suit and air tanks. I'm in." Jose threw himself in there early. "I would suggest two people though. Just in case. You know. Buddy system."

"I got you, bud." Kylar volunteered to be his second.

"Why don't we hold onto that idea for now? I'm not sure you could get them away from that pile now anyway. I think we can run around and grab everything we need without worrying about them."

"Yeah. I can see that. Good idea. I don't wanna be bait until I have to. But I will." They picked ten blocks clean by the end of the day. Never having to budge a zombie.

A middle-aged man came walking up to the fence line of the neighborhood. Nervous and dirty, he looked back and forth constantly. He needed to be a part of the group. Desperately. Lives depended on it. Others would lose theirs in the process but that was a lesser concern for him. He had a mission.

"Hold. What do you want?" One of the guards challenged him.

"I need food and water. I've been walking for days. My family is gone. I'm all alone. Please let me in."

"Stay there." One of the other guards talked into a radio and was told to let him in but take any weapons. No need in letting someone unknown wander around armed in a safe zone. They sent him on to meet some of the locals, so they could get a feel of him. He seemed a little squirrelly but harmless. Once the get-to-know-you was done, they fed him and brought some water. Over the next couple days, he would ingratiate himself and try to be useful.

"Who is the new guy?" William was watching him with a sense of wonder.

"His name is Corey Smith. He says his family was killed on day two and he's been wandering aimlessly since. From Richwood. One of those big money neighborhoods with the Home Owner's Association thing. They probably had no idea how to act when this happened." Davis had been next to William while trying to get some steak ready for the pit.

"What's your read on him?"

"Don't know yet but my hackles rose. Can't put my finger on why though. He doesn't feel threatening in any way."

"Yeah. I'm getting that from here. Ain't even met him yet. I think we've all seen movies where the least expected guy can fuck things up."

Peering over at him again, Davis said, "Right. We better keep an eye on him then."

"That's a big roger. I'm gonna have a couple of the guys watch over him like they do the fence. Twenty-four-hour surveillance for a week should do it."

"Good call. That's why you're second in command."

"Shut up and cook that meat."

Chapter 24

Halloween, Thursday, October 31st

2am Near Fort Hood

The helicopter landed about ten miles away from the military base and shut down. The decisions had been made the night before to recon the area thoroughly before Senator Fred Cruz was to set foot anywhere outside their ready-made safe zone. He was far too valuable to their future and they knew it. Even if Fred wouldn't believe it. So, Peter, Jack, and several other of their friends would hoof it and encompass the main area of Fort Hood. This wouldn't be as hard as most think. Most of the base was for training and exercises. Only a small portion was where people dwelled and worked on a regular basis.

After putting down a few straggling munchers that came to check out the noise with suppressed shots, the eight military operators all moved out and away from the whirly-bird and towards their objective. They all had military comms on, so they could communicate with the pilot and co-pilot. They would stay behind and be ready; watching as the men melted into the tree line.

Silence was maintained the entire hike except for a couple of muted shots. Ten miles was a long way to go and not expect to see an infected out hunting for breakfast. Once they were close to the far edge of the trees, almost exposed to the base, they grouped up to watch. Perimeter fencing, manned guard towers with snipers, and roving patrols inside the base were seen. They were doing a great job of keeping their people safe. Looked like the general knew what he needed to do.

After rechecking their synchronization, they moved out again. Two groups of two down each side of the base. They had already agreed upon where they would each set up. Four corners to get the maximum coverage. One team would have to work their way inside the fencing to get on the backside and near the training areas. This would take extra time and Jack's team would signal when he arrived and was in position. Only very quiet words would be whispered from here on out and only when necessary. One person would try and nap while the other kept watch from here on. Special operators were used to getting sleep when and where they could, so it wasn't hard for the first ones to fall off. Then they just watched and waited. Again, the hardest part. They seem to be doing it a lot lately.

Senator Fred Cruz, John, and the ladies were all on the Bell Huey by nine in the morning; looking forward to meeting the general and the good men and women at Fort Hood. It had been a staple of Texas for a long time. It had even endured a terrorist attack from one of its own years ago. Some dumbass that turned against America after being trained and nurtured in her care. Once again, the government had failed to do its job and protect its citizens, having previous knowledge of the man's radicalization before the tragedy. Afterwards, General Stephen Willoughby was brought in and the majority of this little town's people were happy with the outcome. He was a good man that ruled fair but didn't put up with stupid bullshit. He even went to bat when idiotic rules or regulations came down from the ivory tower that used to be Washington, D.C. Whatever he could do to insulate the men, women, and children under his command, he would.

The helicopter came screeching through the sky while the ladies oohed and aahed over the scenery. Most had not been in one before and were enjoying the view from above. That is until they got near Brenham. The area was overrun with infected. They swarmed and roamed throughout the countryside and small town.

"Damn. I thought I wanted ice cream." John made the comment in jest, but it was a sad sight to see and he knew it. "I'm guessing people were at work when the infected reached Brenham. Look. You see the majority are still near the Blue Bell factory."

They just watched as they continued on towards the base. Nothing they could do. Radioing ahead, they checked in with the recon crew. Everything was going smoothly and there were no problems. They then radioed Fort Hood on their impending arrival. They were still thirty minutes out, but the base was ready for them.

As they came in for a landing, John tried to search out his men along the perimeter, but they were so good at their jobs that it was an impossibility. He smiled. Muttonchop shut down the rotors and they unloaded to a greeting of the local brass. General Stephen Willoughby stood by and shook their hands as they came away from the helicopter pad.

"Good to meet you all, I'm General Willoughby. Please call me Stephen. Welcome to Fort Hood."

"A pleasure, sir. I'm Fred Cruz, this is my wife, Lydia." Shaking hands, Willoughby moved to the next.

"I'm John Parks, this is my girlfriend, Terry, and my partner, Sheila."

"Good to meet you all. Let's move inside and talk." They spent the next few hours discussing various things. Everything was going great and then Willoughby dropped his bombshell on the senator.

"Sir. The real reason I wanted you here is a matter of great importance." He took a couple of seconds and then just spit it out. "We need you to be our acting president."

With a kind of fake surprise on his face, Fred spoke. "Well. There's the rub. I had a feeling you had something like that in mind. John's been dropping hints, too."

"We need a strong leader for everyone to gather around. We may all be running things pretty well right now, but we are all still just individual fiefdoms. If you wanna call us that. We're surviving, basically. This won't last long without a central government of some sort. A leadership role. Too many small dictatorships will never work. Man has proven that it doesn't work for long. Hell, even a centralized government can be a problem with the wrong people running it. Evidenced by Washington D.C. the last several decades." Willoughby got up to grab another cup of coffee.

"I agree with your premise, but I'm not sure if we're ready for it yet. There are too many small groups out there, as you said. Not enough communication between us all on top of it. Most probably won't fall in line with this idea." Taking the offered cup from Stephen, Fred continued. "I don't think a central government could even be established yet. And what if someone else higher up comes along?"

"That would be a problem. I hadn't thought that far ahead. Well, that's not true. I thought about it but dismissed it. Even if someone else was still out there. This is Texas. We control our own destiny. I think our biggest concern, besides being eaten, is if there is another ranking official alive. What if he or she is not as good or even cognitive enough to be in charge." John was deep in thought. This was something that had been discussed only in a cursory examination.

"Each group will have to decide for themselves who will be in charge. We also have to realize that we may never have a central form of government again. Let's face facts. The only way it happened before was because outlying areas were forced into submission by gunpoint and promises. A lot of territories didn't want to give up their freedoms a couple hundred years ago, but their elected officials brought them into the fold and under someone else's thumb. Subterfuge and lies. I don't believe any of us will stand for that. Not this time. It may take years for us to be a country again and even then, it won't be the same." Willoughby let all of this soak in.

"Points made. Well, general. If the people want me to be in charge, I won't say no. I will however require some of you to be my counsel. No arguments. When everyone is ready, I'll do it."

"Good deal. Thank you, Fred."

"Just throwing this out there. I've also had this feeling of impending doom lately. I know my instincts aren't known by you general, but I am usually pretty spot on. Something is brewing. We're only in the second week but we've seen some major activity of the bad guy variety. Ravenhearst looks like they're planning something big. They're too organized, too quickly. Something is going on there. There have also been cartel problems down south. Coast Guard had a run-in with them and I heard from Bert about the Harlingen attack. McAllen is gone too. Completely overrun by infected. We might be seeing more of that as we branch further out. The cartel might be thinking they can take Texas back without much fuss. We're fighting multiple mini-wars to go along with a zombie problem."

"Fill me in on all of that. I've always hated those Ravenhearst shits. What happened?" John spent the next little while filling the general in on Pearland and the massacre. Speculation went around but everyone was definitely wondering what was next.

John excused himself after he finished downloading the general. Calling out to his men around the horn, he found that all was quiet on the perimeter. The helicopter crew were concealed, and all was well there too. So far, so good. He walked back inside for more discussions. He wasn't trying to keep the general out of the loop, just being cautious for now.

Later, one of Willoughby's sergeants came in and informed him on how the party was shaping up for the night. Having not brought any costumes, John and friends would stand out but no one cared. It was to be a fun night anyway and the many children of the families were to be the focus. Some of the families wanted to help make quick costumes or see what they had that would fit for anyone interested. Of course, Sheila jumped into the spirit along with Terry. The next several hours were spent getting to know people and prepping for fun. They would discuss things a little further the next morning.

Chapter 25

Lake Jackson Breakfast time

Over coffee Halloween morning, Michael pulled Steve and Davis aside for a little talk. After each grabbed a plate of eggs, bacon, and some orange juice they walked into the house Michael had been calling home. Once settled in, Michael began.

"I've got a small mission for you two. If you choose to accept it."

"Great. Now he thinks he's Peter Graves." Steve caught onto the Mission Impossible choice of words rather quickly.

"That's exactly what I was going for, but this isn't an impossible mission. I want you to check out Ellington and see what's going on. Take a couple more with you. With how quickly things turned at the airport, I'm a little worried about the Air Force base. If the wrong people have control, that could turn into a clusterfuck for us later."

"I can see that. Now that you mention it, what if Ravenhearst has already been there? It scares me that they are already turning up and causing so much havoc. As if the zombies weren't enough of a problem." Davis took a sip of juice with a concerned look on his face.

"It is starting to look like they knew this was going to happen. That's part of the reason I want to do this now. I talked to Bert and he has had no communication with Ellington or anyone in Galveston. That will be next but not today. There's a lot of different Army and Air Force locations across Texas and some aren't responding to calls. I think that Ravenhearst is acting fast and furious."

Taking a moment, Steve looked up and spoke. "What if they already have Ellington?"

"Don't get seen. I don't want to lose you. Please don't engage unless you have to. I'm actually praying that the Air Force personnel are still there and have no way to communicate or are scared to. I don't really believe that, but it is the slimmest of possibilities. Or even if they just bugged out, it would be better that Ravenhearst wasn't there. Hell. Even if someone else had it, that would be better. We could deal with that"

"All right. Recon only unless the Air Force is actually there. Got it."

"Thanks guys. Grab some volunteers and get moving. I want you back tonight for the festivities. You deserve it as much as everyone else."

"Hell yeah. I like to party." Steve had a big smile on his face.

Returning to the plants the next day proved to be a little harder. Stopped at the top of the bridge as before, they could see another large group of infected heading down the private road and through the gates of Dow. They watched and waited but the line of Zs just kept flowing.

"Shit. Must be feeding time. That hill is a magnet. Kind of wish I had a bomb to drop on it. Would solve a lot of problems." Danny was looking through some high-powered binoculars. "There's too much water on the blocks to not try for but it might be a while before we could get to it. When those zombies get done with that hill, they're going to be looking our way next. We're the only restaurant in town."

"Suggestions?" Aaron was concerned.

"Run them through the chlorine block driving the Kubotas." Jose piped up. He was always a little crazy.

"Say what? I thought we would have to ride bikes or just run. Wouldn't that cause an explosion?"

"Nah. Chlorine's not explosive. The only concern we'll have is plenty of air and if it decides to rain. Rain would turn it to acid. Since we don't have any more weather forecasts, we're taking a chance. It does look ugly up there."

"Don't forget about the Dow bubble. It usually causes all the rain to go around the plant area."

"True. But I still don't wanna be in the middle if it does rain. I'm definitely jumping into a Kubota."

"Any other less nuts suggestion?"

"Shoot them all but we would run out of bullets and have to run. So…no."

"Okay, Jose. Fill us in on how you wanna do this."

Not having any real choice in how to get into the plant, they screeched down the off ramp and into the plant. Zombies followed as quick as they were able, but they outpaced them.

Unfortunately, they were everywhere all the way through the gates and along the roads. All heading toward lunch on the hill. Or at least, they were. Now they had fresher food to focus on. And they were running hell bent for leather after the trucks.

They had decided to drive as fast as possible to the block they had worked and cleared out. They knew where the Kubotas were and the rest could barricade inside the control room. As soon as they got to the block, a couple guys ran to bring over the four wheelers while Jose and Kylar suited up. They only had a precious few minutes, but they would exit out the other side of the building to buy some time. The plan was to split up, each in a different direction, to gather as many as possible.

Jose had the most daunting job. His was to drive over to the hill and circle it till he could gather as many as he was able. He was the first out the back and gone up the road. He drove straight up, honking the little horn over and over to garner attention. He had a pretty good following the first time around while dodging a few. The second time he only got halfway before a gigantic mass of infected came up on over the lip of the hill, flooding after him with blood on their minds. Jose veered off the laid dirt track and bounced down the hillside. Nearly tumbling over the little cart, he went onto the driver's side wheels only. Thinking quickly, he moved all of his weight to the right to get back down and the tires caught again; kicking up dirt and boogying on down to the road again.

Looking in the review mirror, his heart stopped. He really didn't wanna venture a guess on how many of the munchers were behind him, but it had to be in the hundreds. He swallowed a very dry gulp and tried to push the gas pedal down through the floorboard. Jose really didn't wanna die like this. Still several blocks away from Chlorine 7, he took a circuitous route there, trying to gather as many of the infected with him. Radioing Kylar, he relayed his position and timeframe to target.

Kylar might have thought his job would be easier than Jose's, but he found that to be the most overrated statement ever. Leaving the block on his own four-wheeler, he had maneuvered back up near the front gates. For his part, he was to round up all of those still making their way toward the hill, front and back gates both. From the get-go, it was hell. Not even getting close to the front gate, he ran smack into the majority of those that were still trying to chase down their vehicles. They were even coming out of the woods around the gated areas. Determined to get through, even if there were gators in the swamps. As was evidenced by the old man being dragged down by one now. The one funny part was a few of the infected were actually going for the gator itself. Good luck winning that one.

Kylar didn't even bother slamming on the brakes, he just twisted the wheel around and took off through the grass. Once he got to the other side of the next block, he took another turn back toward the plant because there were even more coming from the contractor entrance. Everywhere he turned there were more. Peeling through the gravel parking area, he rolled on down the road towards the other end of the plant itself. It was about a mile across and he still had work to do.

Once he arrived though, there was almost no sign of anything anywhere. Only a couple infected were roaming the Freeport side of Plant B. Maybe the fish and seagulls had kept them busy this way. He turned again, back toward the line of munchers he had left behind in order to round them back up. Just before he reached them, he turned left towards Chlorine 7 himself. That was about the time Jose called him. The others were all listening in from the control room they were stationed in.

Jose would be coming from the south side while Kylar was screaming in from the east. They were going to slow up a little before reaching the block and make sure everything possible was following them to death. They still both had on their air tanks and suits with no worry of not having enough for now. They each had more than ten minutes left of air and proceeded on.

Just as they each got to the edge of the block, Kylar's cart sputtered and died. Out of gas. He tried to turn it back over once, twice, and then jumped out and ran. He wasn't going to be fast, not with a chemical suit and rubber boots on but he gave it his all. The fact he was in the gas helped him and not the infected though. They started coughing and weaving not too far in. Luckily for him, Jose saw him running and veered his way to pick him up. Without stopping, Kylar jumped onto the side seat and was almost dragged out by an infected hand. Trying to run in a suit was still slower than some zombies, even with the shape Kylar was in. The infected man only got one try though as he was already gasping and rasping for air to fill his lungs. But there was none to be had. Only yellowish-green chlorine was in the air and it was thick. Jose turned back toward the north and they left as quickly as the small cart would take them.

Once out the other side, Kylar's air tank started clanging the alarm bell. The extra exertion depleted his air supply. They weren't clear of the tremendous cloud yet, so he had to connect his five-minute escape bottle quickly; while careening away. Jose glanced in the rearview and saw only a couple infected still trying to come after them. A little ways away though. No danger from that front. They were quickly falling out and dying. It could be a very long time before all of the chlorine dissipated, depending on the leak and weather. At least that bit of bad business was done. The two of them had just taken down an unknown amount of infected numbering in the hundreds.

Kylar finally got his air jacked in and was doing fine. That could have been much worse if it had happened just a couple minutes earlier. It would have been a man down situation and there was no way to bring him back out. Finally clearing the clouded area, they rocketed back towards their base block. Kylar radioed ahead of their impending arrival. They screeched to a halt outside the control room door amongst a waiting phalanx of fan club warriors. Holding the fort down with guns out and ready.

Tearing their gear off, they took deep breaths of actual God-made air, pouring buckets of sweat at the same time. And it was a nice sixty-two degrees outside on an overcast day. Going inside, they sat a spell. They still had work to do; gathering more books, water, and any tools that would prove useful later. Kylar and Jose lay on the floor of the control room, comfortable in the knowledge that they have just wiped out a great portion of the chemical plant zombies. For now.

More would come though. That hill was too inviting as a free food source.

After a minute of relaxation, Kylar spoke up. "Note to self. Gas the damn thing up next time. That might have gone a lot smoother." Being in a much safer position, they all broke out in laughter. Take the funny where and when you could.

Chapter 26

Lake Jackson Mall Property

The top of a teenage girl's head went rolling down the staircase, bouncing and careening off the far wall until it finally plopped to a stop on the next landing. The body just collapsed where it died. Gopher One was trying to keep the killing as quiet as possible while he kept running up the steps until he couldn't. The eighth-floor emergency stairwell was filled with more infected than he could handle. Yanking open the next floor's door, he threw himself through it and slammed the door shut; several hands and bodies hit it and made even more noise.

Turning and walking toward the elevators, he punched the up button and waited. This floor was eerily quiet so far. The doors opened and out came another of the newly brainfried. Sidestepping the thirty-something woman, he stuck his foot out and tripped her. Once she was on the ground, he put a knife through her brainpan and then wiped it off on her sundress. Stepping into the elevator without any remorse, he punched the top floor button.

When he first entered the hotel, there had been no chance for him to get near the elevators. Infected had been staying in the lobby area. Conveniently near the kitchen that served breakfast and dinner. Only a couple of the munchers had even seen him as he veered off to the staircase up. Gopher One was trying to get to the roof of this particular hotel. The Courtyard by Marriot was the tallest building in the area that he could observe both the Wal-Mart and neighborhood that the large group was inhabiting. He had a job to do and you either did your allotted job or you suffered the consequences. No quarter.

He made it to the top floor and got out cautiously. Walking the several feet over to the stairs that would take him to the roof, he listened intently. Nothing. The hotel was still fairly new, so he guessed it just didn't have that many guests yet. Pushing open the door to the roof stairs, something snarled behind him and he was shoved through the doors with a massive force. They both fell onto the bottom stairs and Gopher One busted his mouth on them. In a fit of sudden rage, he rolled out from under the behemoth of a man and just started pummeling the overweight older guy all about the face. Hit after hit landed until blood was flying and the man's head was a pile of mush. Still whaling away, his sat phone vibrated. Finally getting control of himself, he wiped off his hands on the man's pants before he answered.

"Yeah."

"That is not how you talk to me. And what took you so long to answer?" Control sounded irate. Easy for them since they weren't out in the thick of things and safe in a nice air-conditioned room.

"I was busy beating the shit out of a very fat zombie."

"You still don't answer that way. I could have destructed you."

"Yeah, yeah. Sorry, okay? I was a little unhappy since he busted my mouth on a staircase."

"Get over it. What were you doing on a staircase? You're supposed to be watching that group."

"I'm trying to get to a higher vantage point so I can watch them all. You do your job and I'll do mine."

"Watch your tone with me. I'm your control."

"No, just the guy I have to talk to this time. You change people every shift. Don't get uppity with me. You're just a cog. And don't ever threaten to blow me up either. You do that with no cause and you know they'll skin you alive. You're just a peon so stow your bullshit. What do you want?"

Changing the way he spoke, knowing that he had screwed up and recovering from it, control said, "Brass wants you to do something new. Try and bring down the group a little."

"Shit. I just got to the top of this damn hotel. What do they want me to do?"

"Find a way to guide some of the infected to their doors. Whatever it takes. Try to get them inside. See how resolved and prepared they are for the unexpected."

"Son of a bitch. Okay. I'll think of something. That it?"

"For now."

"All right."

Hanging up, he walked over to the edge and pulled out his high-powered binoculars. First, he gathered as much intelligence on the Wal-Mart as he could, unbeknownst to him of what was behind it. He had no idea of the 'farm' they had set up, but it wouldn't have mattered anyway for his purposes. Setting the majority of his time elsewhere, he watched over the burgeoning neighborhood. The large community was his priority.

Since he had no way of knowing how fortified or how many people were inside the Wal-Mart, he had to test the defenses of the homes instead. Even trying to get to the helicopter or vehicles would get him killed. They had spotters on the roof and a few roaming the Wally's parking lot outside.

It took a good amount of time, but he finally found something to help him. Forming a makeshift plan in his head, he spent most of the day going back and forth spying. Working out what and how he was going to perform these new actions, he then started on the when. Sometime after midnight maybe. Once they were all nice and snugly in their beds. By early evening, he was ready. Now he just had to get down and the prospect of going down the stairs was not his idea of fun. Fortunately, he had the forethought to bring his rappelling rope. It would be much easier, and more fun, than it had been to get up here.

The trip down F.M. 2004 out to IH 45 was pretty uneventful. They were able to haul ass, going ninety without worrying about cops. Steve even commented along the way about how full of shit the government was trying to say speed limits were for their safety. It was all about making money. Just because some dumbasses can't drive fast doesn't mean you should penalize the entire nation. Davis even piped up with his two cents about how it was further proven by speed limits changing around Houston a few years ago. That had been done because of environmental reasons only. Money. That conversation lasted about half the trip before they cranked up the eighties rock music.

IH 45 was a very different story though. There were vehicles all over. Some on top of each other, multiple accidents had occurred in both directions. Big tractor trailer rigs overturned or jack-knifed blocked major portions along the way. Frequently, they had to drive onto the grass or completely off and onto the feeder roads. Once, it was so bad that they drove over into the shopping center to get around the blocked intersection of the feeder. This particular excursion drew quite a few feverheads along, but they stayed just far enough ahead that it wasn't an issue. They eventually fell off.

As they drew closer to Houston, the worse it got. And slower. Much slower driving. Several infected made their way to the trucks and banged against them, trying to get in. Ignoring them all, they slowly made their way through the abandoned cars. Their pickups were tall enough that they weren't worried about the zombies breaking their windows either. Making it closer, they were within five miles before they had to pull off and start going through the side streets. The highway was too congested and the infected were milling all over around the major intersections and shopping centers. And strip malls were prevalent as you drew closer to Houston. Bumping off freeway and through the grass, they took the first side street they could and maneuvered further north.

It was slow going and GPS was still working on their phones. Mostly. The signal was starting to weaken so instead of 4G, they had maybe a bar of reception. This close to Houston, it shouldn't be a problem, but they guessed some of the towers may be down. Knowing their general direction, they kept trudging along. After several turns of being made to go the wrong direction because of infected infestations, they were able to get back to the feeder road.

Finally making it to Clear Lake Blvd, they turned off to head to Highway 3. This would take them to the Ellington Air Force Base entrance. Still half a mile away, they came to an abrupt stop as they reached 3. A SUV could be seen a couple blocks away with a gunner out the top of it. Not patrolling but definitely a sentry. Steve was driving the first truck, so he waved out the window to back up. He kept having to wave though as the next vehicle didn't know exactly how far back he was wanting. Once they were about a block back, Steve and Davis got out and walked back to talk with their volunteers.

"Hey, guys. I know you're probably wondering, 'What the Hell?' but it's because we saw an armed truck up ahead. Don't know who or anything. Steve and I are going to scout it out. This will take a few hours. I would say either hunker down out of sight or maybe even place yourselves in the woods and watch. That's probably a better idea anyway. I'm thinking we should drive the trucks off the road a little as if they were abandoned. Just in case they patrol this way." Davis was taking the lead as he had a few more years of military than Steve. Even at the plant they had been this way.

"Try and use only silent weapons if you have to take out any infected too. Don't draw attention to yourselves if not necessary. Just keep yourselves safe. We'll find you when we get back but don't expect us anytime soon. No idea how long this till take." Steve tapped the driver's side door frame. He and Davis moved out from there and melted into opposite side woods.

Slowly, the two of them moved past the armed sentry vehicle through the woods. There were no markings on it, so they still had no idea who was in control. It looked armored and the man on top was a professional. Constantly scanning. Once past it, they continued as close to the entrance as they could get. Which wasn't far away. Whoever they were, they were comfortable enough with their sentries in place that no guards were roaming around outside.

Staying on the opposite side of the little highway, using binoculars, they went into reconnaissance mode. Their vision was limited from this side, but they noted many people milling about around the base. Definitely not Air Force but still no distinctive sight of who. After thirty minutes and all they could note, they started moving around the side of the base. Slow going again, they picked through fallen limbs and trees until they were in a good spot to have an overview.

"Damn. Who are these guys? They're organized but I don't see them doing anything with the hardware." Steve whispered.

"Yeah. Kind of like they're just the watchdogs. The guys who have to stay guard but have no idea what to do with the stuff. I wish we could tell if they were good or bad guys though. No actual uniforms, just normal black BDUs (battle dress uniform)."

"They've even got roving patrols inside the fence line. They know what they're doing as far as security. Except for people like us, of course."

"Yeah. Definitely ready for any normal try at breaking in or even a semi-heavy zombie run at them. These guys have training. Either military, police, or major corporate security type. This is bad." Peering again, he caught a glimpse of something big inside one of the hangers. "Shit. It's Ravenhearst. Look. Inside Hanger 2. Big Lear jet has their logo. Must be someone important here running the show. Fuck. This is really bad." Davis was writing in his little notebook everything he could see. They might need it later. "Let's get the fuck out of here."

"Roger that."

It took them almost another hour to sneak their way back through the woods while staying out of sight and silent. Catching up with their backup, they got moving again. Deciding to fill them in later with the rest of the group, it was a very solemn ride home for Steve and Davis. Every once in the while one of them would venture an idea of what might be going on, but the fear was readily seen on both of their faces. This would probably be very, very bad for them.

When they arrived back in Lake Jackson, Steve and Davis made a bee-line for Michael. They grabbed everyone from their original group they saw along the way. It was early evening and the Halloween decorations and festivities were almost ready. Most were awaiting a fun time that was badly needed for many, but Michael's new household was fixing to be full of some very bad news. They were able to gather William, Alberto, Warren, Terry, Germ, and even Sam and Penelope. Once they were settled in the living room, Davis began.

"Bad news my friends. Ellington is in the hands of Ravenhearst. We saw no sign of Air Force personnel. I can only hope they got away and not killed."

"Shit. I was really praying that wouldn't be the case. More and more, it looks like they knew this virus was going to happen ahead of time. They were too ready to move in on key places." Michael rubbed his chin with concern.

"They have sentries set up too. I assume at all points around the base. We saw a heavily armored SUV with a gunner where we came up. No one is moving them out from there any time soon. The only good news for now is that it didn't look as if anyone there knew how to fly or work any of the equipment yet. Except for maybe the one pilot of the Lear. No worry today at least but we're going to need help against them if it comes down to it."

"All right. We'll have to brainstorm some possibilities then. Maybe Bert can somehow help but he's a long way from here in a pinch. Anything else?"

"Just that 45 is a gigantic mess. Really hard sledding. Rigs, cars, trucks; you name it and it is in the way. Lots of accidents and plenty of infected too. Not worth trying to drive it, either way."

"Awesome. Well. That's a problem for tomorrow, I guess. Everyone get out of here and prepare for tonight. We have a party to make great for the children, at least. They don't need every day to be doom and gloom. I think a few of them planned on being *World of Warcraft*, *Elder Scrolls*, and even anime characters. I don't know much about anime at all, but I saw a couple of the muscle suits from *Attack on Titan*. I actually watched the first season. Crazy stuff. There was also talk from the older teenagers about orcs, pandas, or even worgen costumes. That should be cool. Some of these kids are pretty good at putting stuff together. They've helped out with torn clothing and things like that. Enough from me, we'll talk more tomorrow." With that, they all slowly moved out of the house. Each of them would let others know of the goings on along the way.

Preparations for the night were going on across South Texas; Lake Jackson, Alvin, Timmons's farm in Corpus Christi, John's Houston base, and even Fort Hood. Each of the areas had sentries on duty while everyone else put on their costumes, got ready for children in makeshift haunted houses, helped with dinner, or just put the candy out at building entrances, guard shacks, and at various homes with an adult to delve it out. The gym at the Alvin High School was turned into a small maze of horror for the few there. All of the adults at the Timmons's farm had kept the children away from the barn for the last couple days. They were ready to scare the poop out of the massive amount of kids from the Corpus base and the U.S.S. Lexington aircraft carrier.

Children and adults had been shipped over to the farm for the last couple days; ever since Bert and crew had been there. Along with the costumes and candy found. Some of the men had decided a week ago to start taking missions to every school in the Corpus Christi area. It was a daunting task, but they knew there still had to be surviving children in some of them. The longer they waited, the less likely they would live. And they were right. A great many more were found amongst the various buildings. At some it was just a few, and at others it numbered into the hundred plus category.

The horror they witnessed while performing these mercy missions weighed on the soldiers each day. Tasked with having to put down many more children and adults than they saved was a very heavy burden. Being part of the once greatest military ever, possibly only one left, these men and women took this burden upon themselves and did what was needed of them.

Saving lives was the greatest of priorities and they excelled where able. In fact, even on this day of celebration for most, the crews were out again. Going even further than before, they were on one last outing to the Tuloso-Midway Primary School. It was the last in the greater Corpus area. That was how dedicated they were. A dozen and a half schools cleared out in the last five days. They were really hoping they could make a few more children's days by saving them and getting them to the party. Every person thanked the good men and women of the American forces. Doing what needs to be done as it needs to be done.

The trip had been quick and easy to the grade school, but their arrival was marred with sadness. Only a few infected were even in the vicinity but the front doors were broken and shattered. Once inside, they found only more that made their eyes water. Torn apart pieces of children littered the corridors and blood splattered hallways. Viscera and crimson were the only things to be found for them. Checking every office, bathroom, and class area didn't help. Nothing alive moved or whimpered.

"All right, people. Let's get out of here. I can't take much more of this." The Marine in charge got his volunteers moving towards the front doors. Then he stopped. And listened really hard.

"Do you here that? Sounds like crying."

"Coming from the ceiling, sir."

"Everyone, take positions." They each trained their weapons toward the air ducts. "Come down from there. We won't hurt you." The crying just kept going.

Poking where he thought the person might be with his rifle, he spoke again. "It's okay. No infected are here. You can come down."

Movement started slowly and then picked up. The air ducts started shaking and straining the holders. Following along, they kept talking to the person to calm them, but it was no use. Suddenly, the ducts hangers broke, and a four-foot section came tumbling down. A young woman of about five foot nothing slowly got up. Crying and laughing at the same time, she shook in place. Then, suddenly, she took off. Running for all she was worth, she was out the front doors and gone before any of them could react.

"What the hell was that?" One of the other members asked.

"Some people break in mysterious ways. Move out. Nothing left for us here." With that, they all loaded up. Driving off, the commanding officer began to cry. Silently and to himself. The others noticed but said nothing. Each living through their own pain and continuing on.

Chapter 27

Alvin, TX.

Charles and Angelica were still heading towards the Alvin Police Department. It had been days of slow moving and not eating much along the way. Surviving was hard, but they were determined to live. The sun was starting to wax and wane towards the far end of the western horizon. Maybe an hour till it would be dark, they needed to find shelter now. No sense in running around waiting for an infected child to sneak up on them and bite an ankle in the dark. They were a block away from the station when they immediately stopped before turning the next corner. Someone was out there.

They could see a dozen military types milling about. A few were toting armfuls of munitions from out of the building. Several large crates lugged in pairs of two and loaded onto big trucks. The uniforms were a little off though. They were completely black with no insignias of any kind. Not U.S. military from the looks. Could be black ops but they didn't seem right.

Charles was a partial conspiracy theorist and started to speculate on who they were. He figured either Blackwater, Secure-Mil, or Ravenhearst. They were the only ones with the juice to be this well-organized this quickly. Blackwater had never operated like this on American soil and Secure-Mil had always been a very tight-shipped group. One of the only of its kind with a squeaky-clean reputation. As clean as you could get anyway. They would drop or help prosecute any who got out of line. That left Ravenhearst. Their reputation was on the opposite side of clean, but they always skated because of the types of friends in high places they had. Even further speculation was that a bigger group was behind them, but no one knew who they were.

Angelica watched their backs with a small pistol while Charles continued his surveillance. An occasional shot took out an infected as they wandered into the area. Muffled shots. Sound suppressors were on the end of every rifle he saw. They had come prepared, knowing there would be zombies that had to be shot. After a while, they finished up and moved out. In the direction of the high school, only about a mile away. Charles didn't know where they were going at the time or that there were survivors there, but he and Angelica weren't about to follow. They needed help but tonight the abandoned police station was a good place to hole up for the night. The doors weren't broken so they were able to close and lock them up tight. Settling down they pulled out the last of their food and had some water before rolling out their bedrolls and falling asleep.

Sheriff Billy Ingram came in the back door with a giant box full of costumes for the smaller children. Many of them had been decorating the gymnasium for the last couple hours while a couple groups ran out to various stores. The idea was to find as many different costumes and decorations as they could. There were many children here at the high school and the adults thought it would be a good idea to try and make at least one night pleasant for them. It was Halloween and it might be the last time they got candy. A party was ready to be had.

The adults had kept all of the children under sixteen out of the gym. Wanting to keep them in the dark. Knowing some were mature enough despite their age, a few younger ones were helping out, trying to make it as scary as they would like it. One giant haunted house with a small open area for refreshments was the plan. Ingram brought in his box along with several other people's boxes behind him. Some of the older 'kids' had been working on their get-ups for a few days now. Not like there was a lot of other things to do. Everyone was going to have a great time tonight. At least those not on guard duty.

"One-eyed Jack to Mr. Rogers. Come in."

"Go for Rogers. What's your status?"

"I have eyes on targets. Big high school. Going to take multiple entries but not much opposition. A few guards watching; one on each entrance. Lot of glass. They're throwing a party tonight."

"Yeah. Halloween. Let them have it. We'll hit them in the middle of the night."

"Sir. There are a lot of women and children in there. Innocents. Only about a dozen men total. Some of them cops."

"The innocents will live unless they get in the way. You know our orders. We take all the weapons from everyone. Doesn't matter who or where. If someone gets in the way, they get put down. Permanently. That's the way it is. Are you good or do you need to be relieved?"

After a second of swallowing his apprehension, he spoke. "I'm good, sir."

"Okay then. Let them have their fun, for tonight is the last time they have that opportunity. We are a few more minutes away. The station is cleared. Looks like the cops took everything they could with them but there was still a shitload of the bigger munitions. Stay on them."

"Copy that, sir." One-eyed Jack signed off and started to tear up. This is not what he wanted to be doing but he knew the consequences of disobeying at Ravenhearst. You didn't live to do it again. Innocent people were fixing to die. All because someone wanted to be in control of everything.

Gopher One killed the bike engine and started to roll it along the road. The motorcycle was relatively quiet but there was no use in alerting anyone to his presence ahead of time. Not like anyone could have heard him. The noise from the party would have drowned him out. They weren't trying to be loud but when you have that many children and then factor in some alcohol, it still stirred up some sound. The guards were having to take a few shots here and there because of it, but they didn't mind. It was nice to see the children having fun.

He found a good spot within a block of the Lake Jackson neighborhood fencing and set the kickstand. With plenty of time till the midnight hour, he walked at a slow pace and lit a cigar. Only encountering a few infected along the way, he was able to make quick work of them.

Arriving at his destination about two miles down the road, he climbed into the abandoned mini-bus that used to be for public transportation. Starting it up by hot-wiring it, he checked the gas gauge and found there was plenty for his plan. Driving off, he made sure not to go anywhere near the neighborhood and once he was on Highway 288 South, he kicked into gear to the next exit down.

Pulling off the ramp, he veered over immediately and took the first side road. It was a little past where he wanted to go but he didn't want anyone watching from Wal-Mart to know where he went. If they saw him. That little bit of driving would have given him a ticket, or an accident, but really. Who gave a damn now? Gopher smiled at that thought.

Cranking the bus up to the front door of Best Buy, he backed it right into the front doors and through to the sales floor. He hadn't thought about an alarm. Oops. But it didn't go off. Looking around, he realized why. The store had been relatively stripped clean of anything that could still be useful. Computers, televisions, DVDs, and anything of entertainment value. His logical guess was the group scavenged for the children and to have something to do.

Giving things a few minutes to settle, he listened in case he had any company. Either in the store or a new customer. Nothing stirred. Good. He moved off to the car stereo aisle. A plan in his mind, he got to work. It would take him a few hours to complete.

"Hey, Steph. Look at that."

"Hold on. Be right there." Steph walked over to Liv's watch point on top of Wal-Mart. "What?"

"Look. On the freeway. Is that a bus?"

"Yeah. Hauling ass, too." Looking through some binoculars, Steph could see a handsome man at the wheel. Looking behind him, she saw nothing. "Damn, he's hot. I don't see anything chasing him, but he is flying."

"Hey, he just got off at Oak Drive. Damn, he almost flipped that thing. What the hell is he doing?"

"He just went down that road by Home Depot. He's gone."

"Yeah. I don't see him anymore either. That was weird. Oh, well. I'm sure that's not the last time we'll see him."

"I hope not. I wouldn't mind taking a ride on that. Yum."

"Oh, my gawd. You're so bad. Get back to your side, you ho."

"What? It's been a while. You know. If you weren't married, you'd want some of that, too."

"Shut up, you." They laughed a little while Steph went back to her side of the roof.

After the party had wound down and most had gone to bed, the guard rotation changed. It was about midnight and few of the adults were still meandering around the streets. Drinking some spirits and enjoying each other's company. Just before the last crew left, a strange sound rose up in the distance.

"Can you hear that? Almost sounds like music."

"Yeah."

"I can't tell what it is though. Not really. It's like the sound is being warped by the wind." A few more minutes went by while the four of them at the northern most gate pondered what and where that was coming from.

"It's getting more distinct. Maybe louder?"

"Damn. It sure is. I can understand it now. I know that tune."

"That's that *'Ride of the Valkyrie'* song, right?"

"Yeah, it is. Shit. This ain't good. What dumbass is doing this? They're going to attract attention."

"Definitely louder. It's coming this way." Another minute went by before a sudden and scary realization came upon him. "Oh, hell. Hey. Go! Wake everyone! Now! Go! Go!"

The distinctive outline of a rather large vehicle could be seen as it rounded a corner two blocks down and directly in front of the gate. It wasn't going fast but was determinably heading their way. Three of the four ran. Rather quickly, too. One went straight to Michael's, the second to William's home, and the last ran down the road to the next street where Steve and Davis were lounging and drinking. Just before they got to the separate homes, the last guard started yelling.

"Everyone, take cover! Grab your guns! It's coming through!" He jumped down from his wooden outpost and started running back to the houses. "Someone is driving a bus straight at us! And it's bringing infected! A lot!"

'God help us all' was the last thought he had as the gate burst apart from the tons of metal barreling through.

www.ingramcontent.com/pod-product-compliance
Lightning Source LLC
Chambersburg PA
CBHW051523260626
47170CB00003B/752